THE AGE OF INNO-SCENTS
A NORA BLACK MIDLIFE PSYCHIC MYSTERY
BOOK 6

RENEE GEORGE

BARKSIDE OF THE MOON PRESS

PRAISE FOR RENEE GEORGE

"Sense and Scent Ability by Renee George is a delightfully funny, smart, full of excitement, up-all-night fantastic read! I couldn't put it down. The latest installment in the Paranormal Women's Fiction movement, knocks it out of the park. Do yourself a favor and grab a copy today!"

— —ROBYN PETERMAN NYT BESTSELLING AUTHOR

"I'm loving the Paranormal Women's Fiction genre! Renee George's humor shines when a woman of a certain age sniffs out the bad guy and saves her bestie. Funny, strong female friendships rule!"

— -- MICHELLE M. PILLOW, NYT & USAT BESTSELLING AUTHOR

"I smell a winner with Renee George's new book, Sense & Scent Ability! The heroine proves that being over fifty doesn't have to stink, even if her psychic visions do."

— -- MANDY M. ROTH, NY TIMES BESTSELLING AUTHOR

"Sense & Scent Ability is everything! Nora Black is sassy, smart, and her smell-o-vision is scent-sational. I can't wait for the next Nora book!

— —MICHELE FREEMAN, *AUTHOR OF HOMETOWN HOMICIDE, A SHERIFF BLUE HAYES MYSTERY*

Acknowledgments

A huge thank you to my "you saved my butt once again" crew of BFFs Robbin, Michele, and Robyn for hanging in there with me until the very end. Thank you for being my people! I love you guys!

To my editor Kelli Collins. You are a great friend and my rock! I'm sorry I am such a crap client. LOL (The woman is a saint, people!)

To the PWF #13 - Thanks for bringing attention to heroines of a certain age. You ladies are magnificent.

My husband Steve and my son Taylor for taking up the slack around the house, and most of all, leaving me alone to write! I literally couldn't do this without you.

My BFF Dakota Cassidy for being my one true heart when it comes to all things binge-worthy. I love you, girl!

And finally, to the readers. You are making this midlife writer happier than you can even imagine! Thank you for loving Nora and going on this journey with her and her BFF brigade.

The Age of Inno-Scents

A Nora Black Midlife Psychic Mystery Book 6

Copyright © 2022 by Renee George

All rights reserved. No part of this publication may be reproduced, stored in a retrieval system, or transmitted, in any form or by any means, without the prior permission in writing of the copyright holder.

Any trademarks, service marks, product names or named features are assumed to be the property of their respective owners, and are used only for reference. There is no implied endorsement by the author of this work.

This is a work of fiction. All characters and storylines in this book are inspired only by the author's imagination. The characters are based solely in fiction and are in no relation inspired by anyone bearing the same name or names. Any similarities to real persons, situations, or incidents is purely coincidental.

A version of this book was previously published in the **Aged to Perfection Anthology February 2022. ***The Age of Inno-Scents*** has since been expanded with additional content.

Print ISBN: 978-1-947177-43-7

Publisher: Barkside of the Moon Press

My name is Nora Black, and I'm proof-positive that life past fifty just keeps getting better. I have great friends, own my own business, and I have a wonderful man in my life who loves me, crow's feet and all.

For my BFF Gilly's birthday, we are heading to an 80s-themed mystery weekend set in an old high school, and I'm looking forward to big shoulder pads and even bigger hair. The fact that my guy Ezra looks great in tight jeans doesn't hurt one bit, either.

But when my scratch-n-sniff psychic gift acts up, and it sniffs out an actual murderous plot, our fun outing takes a totally deadly turn.

My scent-o-rama is spazzing out to the max!

The clues are in the past, and we're racing against the clock to turn back time. But with my nose for clues and a little luck, hopefully, we can find a killer before schools out for murder.

CHAPTER ONE

When I walked out of the bathroom, Ezra Holden, Detective Hottie, aka the man I loved, slid on a gray Members Only jacket. While his jeans weren't so tight I could see London or France, they did hug his butt in the most delicious way.

"Duuude," I said. "You have a bodacious booty."

He chuckled as he pushed the twin beds together to make one big bed, then turned around to face me. He had a month's worth of beard and mustache going on that I still hadn't gotten used to.

His brows rose as his bright green gaze landed on mine. "Wow, Nora. Those bangs are gravity-defying."

I patted the top of my hair. "Courtesy of freeze spray."

Fortunately, I'd had my roots touched up earlier

in the week, or this ode to 1980s style would've been a no-go. As it was, I'd used enough hairspray that if someone flicked a lighter too close, my hair would become Aqua Net flambé.

I went up on my toes as he dipped his head. His lips brushed mine in a way that made my entire body sing. He slid his hands over my hips and pulled me close, my stomach pressed against his straining groin. "I can't believe this is the first time we've been alone in two weeks."

"That'll teach you to go off undercover with the Feds," I told him. I cupped my fingers behind his neck and twirled the sandy-blond curls that had gotten longer since he'd begun working with the joint drug task force. "I'm so happy you made it back in time for this weekend." I sighed as he pressed his forehead against mine. "But I would've understood if you'd decided to stay home."

He caressed my cheek. "What? And miss you in a ruffled mini dress with the biggest shoulder pads I've ever seen? Not on your life."

"This old thing?" I said coyly, batting my fake eyelashes at him. My dress was golden yellow and was the exact one I'd worn to the winter semi-formal in 1986. After my mom died, I'd found several of my outfits in wardrobe bags hanging in the closet of my girlhood bedroom. The dress was a bit tighter in the waist and hips than it had been when I was seventeen, but thanks to the miracle that is shapewear, it still fit. "I can't believe I have a legit reason to wear it again."

He gave me a quirky half-smile. "It's fun seeing you get all I-love-the-eighties for a weekend. Although, I was surprised they made us give up our cellphones."

School's Out for Murder, Incorporated was a new murder mystery immersive weekend venue in an old renovated high school outside of Button Falls, about forty minutes from Garden Cove. The owner-operators had strict rules about no technology that included laptops, tablets, and phones. I'd done a couple of escape rooms, so I understood the reasoning. Still, I felt a little naked without my cell. The nice thing, though, was that Ezra couldn't get called back to Garden Cove for any reason. After his long absence, I was glad to have him primarily to myself for two days.

"I guess they don't want anyone cheating," I mused.

He smirked. "I'm a detective. I already have an unfair advantage."

"Only if you think applying cop logic to a fictional mystery is an advantage."

Ezra snorted. "We'll see who solves the murder first."

"Hey." I leaned into him. "We're partners in this."

"In all ways," he said before lifting me off the ground and carrying me across the room.

I giggled as he lowered me to the bed.

Until my ass slid between the mattresses.

"This is so not going to work," I said with a laugh.

He shook his head. "They really did a great job of converting these classrooms into guest quarters, but they definitely didn't make them couple-friendly."

"Hah. Maybe that's the point." I unwedged myself from the crevice. "It's a school." The brick walls had been painted a silver-sage color, making the room feel less institutional. "But I bet we can get creative."

"Oh?" The corners of his eyes crinkled as he grinned down at me. "I'm all for creative."

I patted the bed. "I know you are."

He sat down next to me. "Maybe we should skip the dance..." He playfully nipped my lower lip as his fingers danced down the middle of my back. He frowned. "Where's the zipper?"

"It's on the side."

He nuzzled my neck while he explored my dress with his hands. "Interesting…"

The sound of the zipper unzipping was followed by my grateful exhale as the bodice relaxed and gave me more breathing room.

"I think we're going to be a little late," I said.

His warm palm splayed across my ribs as his fingers slid under my bra. He kissed up the side of my neck, the brush of his beard and the heat of his breath pulling strings of pleasure through me. I leaned my head back and moaned.

I felt his satisfied smile against my skin. "We're going to be a lot late."

"I'm good with that."

Three sharp knocks elicited a sound close to a growl from Ezra. "Go away," he said.

"Come on, you guys," Gilly yelled from the other side of the door. "Let's go."

I sighed as Ezra lowered his forehead to my chest. "We have to go, don't we?" he asked.

"It's her birthday," I said. "So, that's a big yes."

When Gilly had found out *School's Out for Murder, Incorporated* was doing a 1980s-themed mystery for their opening weekend, she'd immediately reserved six spots. It hadn't taken much for Pippa Hines—the third in our bestie trio—and me to get on board with the plan. Gilly was turning fifty-four, and her children, twins, were college-aged now and were no longer living at home. In other words, empty nest syndrome was real. To lift Gilly's spirits, we'd been down for whatever was going to make her happy.

I'd closed Scents & Scentsability, the boutique where I sold organic beauty products that I created and curated, for the weekend. Garden Cove was a seasonal tourist town, so we relied mostly on outside orders to keep our profits in the black during the winter months. Pippa, who used to be my assistant when I worked for one of the largest beauty suppliers in the United States, managed the front of the shop. As for Gilly, she was an established massage therapist with twenty years of experience. Honestly, her local clients were our best year-round customers. Getting her to come work with Pippa and me had not only been a good best friend move it had also been great for business.

Gilly knocked again. "Are you coming?"

"Apparently not," Ezra muttered.

I snickered. "We'll be there in a couple of minutes." Long enough for me to get zipped up and Ezra to lose his, uhm, disappointment.

Ezra held up his hand and flashed me five fingers three times in a row.

"Be there in fifteen minutes," I amended.

"Five! And not a minute later. You hear that, Easy?" Gilly said, using Ezra's nickname.

"Why am I in trouble?" he asked.

"Because she knows you about as well as I do."

Ezra winked at me. "You'd be amazed at what I can do in five minutes."

"Settle down, *Risky Business*. This hair and this dress will take longer than five minutes to put back together."

"Fine." He got up and helped me to my feet.

I sucked in my gut and zipped my dress. "We'll sneak away later tonight."

"Promises, promises."

I grabbed him by the collar of his Members Only —not a euphemism—and tugged him close for a kiss. "One I intend to keep." I let him go and walked to the door. "But until then, we have a dance to go to, followed by a mystery to solve." I slid on a pair of yellow Converse low tops. I was not cramming my feet into a pair of bright-colored chunky heels for the sake of authenticity. Besides, Converse were just as popular then as they are now, and my feet would thank me for it later.

"Cute shoes," Ezra said.

I went up on my toes and turned my ankle to him. "I'll have you know that my favorite shoes in the eighties were a pair of high-tops in just this color."

He smiled. "I think they're, like, totally awesome."

"Aw! I didn't know you were a Valley Girl."

"A Valley what?" He shook his head. "There's a whole page devoted to 1980s slang in our check-in packet. I studied it while you were getting ready." He put his arm around me. "Do you think they'll have food?"

I gave his belly a tap. "You had a double cheeseburger and large fries on the way here."

He frowned. "You ate some of my fries."

I held up two fingers. "Two fries."

"I feel like I haven't eaten in weeks."

"Tapeworm," I said.

He frowned as he opened the door. "You're not funny."

I laughed. "I really am."

He bumped shoulders with me. "Spaz."

"Dork," I countered. "Let's boat."

"Huh?"

"Motor on, dude."

"Duuude," he said with a grin. "After you."

When I stepped out into the hall, an older middle-aged man, wearing jeans and a t-shirt, hustled past me. He smelled like he'd been picking herbs in a dank forest of pine trees. In other words, like Drakkar Noir, which could've been called What High School Boys Smelled Like in the 1980s. Mr. Rude clipped me with his shoulder and sent me stumbling sideways against the white lockers lining the walls.

"Hey!" Ezra shouted. I grabbed his arms to keep myself upright, preventing him from going after the rude jerk.

The man gave us a one-finger wave without looking back as he continued his fast walk down the hall.

While the guy was gone, the sweet, herbal scent of his cologne lingered...along with a memory.

"Pizza face," a guy wearing a yellow and blue letter jacket says as he slams another guy into a locker. He has BF in large letters on one side of the jacket, covered in silver and brass letter pins for football, basketball, and baseball. On the other side is a bearded Viking head with a horned hat. Probably the school mascot. The left sleeve has the number ten on his upper arm. The teenager's dark, short-cropped hair is damp, but his face, like those of all his friends and the boy against the locker, is a blur. The pungent aroma of cologne and body spray is heavy in the air.

The hallway is similar to the one we're in now, only it's painted yellow with gray lockers. The speaker's friends, also wearing letter jackets, laugh as each of them gives the kid a shove as they pass by, calling him names.

"Dickbag."

"Douche."

"Dumbass."

The boys are as alliterative as they are cruel.

A woman shouts, "Get to class before I report you all. You won't be laughing when you're benched on Friday night's game."

"Chillax," the instigator says as the rest of the teenagers leave. The bully follows after them, and the kid they've tortured throws his books on the floor and slams his locker shut.

My smell-o-vision, as my best friend Gilly called it, faded.

"Whoa," I said as the sage-green halls and white lockers reappeared. "That was intense."

Ezra had his arm around me, holding me steady. "A vision?"

"Yeah," I said. "A strong one." After dying for twenty-seven seconds during my hysterectomy a little over two years ago, I'd returned to the living with a nose that could literally smell memories. Only, they weren't my memories. The psychic remembrances always belonged to someone else. And they were always tied to aromas that evoked strong emotions. Which meant—thankfully—the memories weren't always about murder and violence. Sometimes they were about moments of pure joy, love, pride, and a myriad of other emotional remembrances that scents could evoke. I couldn't quite put my finger on which mood had triggered this last memory.

"Bad?" Ezra asked.

I nodded again. "No, but yes." I still felt out of sorts.

"Bad enough to make it a police thing?"

I leaned my head against his shoulder, my crispy bangs smooshing against his bearded face. "Do you have a DeLorean I don't know about?"

Ezra arched his brow. "You want to go back to the future?"

"Brushing up on your eighties' movies, I see."

"*Great Scott*, Nora," he teased. "I had the entire DVD collection when I was a kid. I've watched the movies multiple times over the years."

"On DVD, huh?" I'd been a junior in high school when the first movie had released in theaters. And the original videos had come out on VHS tapes. I didn't want to think about how many years after its release Ezra had owned the collection. I waved my hand. "Anyhow, the memory I saw was about a school bully when this place was still Button Falls High, so even if we had a time machine, there's not much we could do about it now."

He pulled me into his arms again and kissed me stupid. With a crooked smile, he said, "Nora Black, I'm so thankful *my density has brought me to you.*" The line was from *Back to the Future,* when George approaches Lorraine in the diner. Only, Ezra said it with such a sweet sincerity it made my heart squeeze. Then he kissed me again in a way that made me want to shove him back inside the room.

"Hah," I replied breathlessly as I patted his chest. "We better get going, McFly."

He wiggled his brows. "I'll grab the plutonium."

CHAPTER
TWO

"Electric Avenue" spilled out of the open gymnasium doors. I started bouncing to the familiar beat. A guy dressed in a powder-blue tuxedo, sporting an A Flock of Seagulls-style hairdo, including spiked sides and a long swath of bangs down in his face, stood outside the doors. He was talking to a woman in a white suit jacket with huge shoulder pads, a black and white polka dot chemise with a black pencil skirt, and white patent leather pumps. Definitely more stylish than anyone I went to school with in the '80s. Her medium-length hair was styled in big, bold curls, making her more Joan Collins than Joan Jett.

"I think I'm underdressed," Ezra said.

"You're perfect."

Next, we saw a jock with a mullet, two cheerleaders—a blonde and brunette—along with a man in tan slacks and a cardigan, congregating on the other side of the corridor. The cheerleaders wore white cheer sweaters with a big green C on the chests and short green skirts. The man who'd shoved past me walked through the double doors blocking off the opposite hallway. He joined the group and put his hand on the brunette cheerleader's arm. She tugged away, and the jock leaned in and said something that made the older man scowl.

"Interesting," I whispered to Ezra. "I bet those are the actors."

"They seem tense," he noted.

"They could be rehearsing. Or it's opening-night jitters, maybe."

He leaned over and kissed my cheek. "Maybe."

The woman with fancy hair smiled at us and gestured toward the open doors. From a distance, she'd looked young-ish, maybe late twenties, early thirties, but up close, I noticed that her unlined forehead didn't have much movement—a classic sign of Botox. Even so, she looked great.

She gave us a stern smile and said, "Go on in, students. Enjoy the dance."

The woman was playing the role of teacher chaperone, and even though it was pretend, for a second, I felt like a schoolgirl. I grabbed Ezra's hand and dragged him inside to what can only be described as an arts and crafts winter wonderland. In other words, it was delightful. The gym ceiling was covered with white and light blue crepe streamers dripping with paper snowflakes. In the center was a mirror ball reflecting white light across the polished wood floor. There were about thirty other guests out on the floor in full '80s regalia, dancing to the funk-reggae hit.

A punch table was set up on the right side, covered in a white tablecloth with blue plastic cups stacked near three large see-through drink dispensers. It was a bit too modern for the '80s, but I let it slide because the containers were definitely more hygienic than an open punchbowl. Centered on the back wall of the gym was a DJ dressed in a bright yellow and electric-blue nylon jogging outfit finished off with a yellow fedora. He had a pair of headphones on as he danced behind his stand.

Gilly, wearing the cutest puffy-sleeved, ruched red dress, waved at us. If my bangs were gravity-defying, Gilly's were orbiting the moon.

"Oh, my gawd!" I squealed. We did an old handshake we'd come up with during our junior year of high school that ended on a fake joint toke. Not that we did a lot of drugs in our teens. It was just something that we thought made us look cool at the time. "You are totally bitchin'."

"No doy," she responded with a twirl and a hair flip. She was wearing red pointy-toed pumps with low heels.

Scott Graham, Gilly's date, wore a white blazer with a scooped-neck blue t-shirt, white pleated pants, and a slick pair of blue and silver penny loafers. Scott was a local surgeon in our hometown of Garden Cove. Gilly had been going out with the hot doc since the fall, and I had a feeling it was getting serious between the two of them.

Pippa and her husband, Jordy Hines, who were both born in the '80s, *ahem*, joined our group. The thirty-something-year-olds had embraced the decade, though. Jordy wore a red leather jacket with tight black and red color-blocked leather pants. He had his long brown hair down around his shoulders, and frankly, his vibe screamed big hair band. Pippa wore a fabulous curly wig that reminded me of a perm I had through most of the '80s, even into college. Her dress was made from fuchsia-colored satin with a lace neckline like Molly Ringwald's dress in *Pretty in Pink*.

"Wowza, Pips. That's freaking awesome." I whistled. "Did you make that yourself?"

She laughed. "I wish I was that talented. I got it from an online shop. It's good, right?"

I nodded. "It's totally boss."

"We're going to start a drinking game," Jordy said. "Every time one of you says 'totally,' we take a swig."

"That's an excellent way to end up with alcohol poisoning," Scott said. "I'm in."

Gilly tilted her head sideways. "Totally."

Pippa and I snickered. We knew Jordy was joking. He didn't drink. Ever. He'd been in Narcotics Anonymous for over twelve years, and while he wasn't an alcoholic, he'd told me once that alcohol lowers inhibitions, making it easier to justify doing drugs. That was something he wasn't willing to chance. There was too much for him to lose. He'd been looking at Pippa when he'd said it.

"When is this thing getting started?" Ezra asked.

I quirked up a brow. "Eager for murder, huh?"

He shook his head then winked at me. "I'm eager for something else, darling. It's been a very long two weeks."

The opening guitar licks to "What I Like About You" by The Romantics poured out of the speakers. "This is my jam," Gilly said excitedly. She grabbed Scott's hand. "Come dance with me."

He willingly went with her, which put points in his column for me. Gilly had a troubled past when it came to men. See: asshole ex-husband. So, I was thrilled that Scott was turning out to be the nice guy he had seemed from the beginning. Gilly whipped her hair around to the new wave jam, her face a beacon of pure joy. It was times like this that I thought my BFF was possibly the most beautiful person I knew. By the look on Scott's face, I was pretty sure he felt the same way I did.

A couple stood near the punch bowl. The attractive woman wore a lime-green tank top with a pink and yellow tutu, pink leg warmers, and clear Jellies. She had a multitude of colorful bangles adorning both her wrists. She tugged at her side ponytail. The guy she was with wore black jeans and a jacket that looked like it had been bought at a Michael Jackson memorabilia sale. His hair was styled in a Rick Astley pompadour. They looked late thirties to early forties, and I was impressed with their commitment to looking commercially '80s.

Pippa sucked in a noisy gasp of air. "That's Nellie Lox." She pointed to the Rick-and-Madonna-looking couple. "I have her channel saved on my Pinstabook account. She does these great makeup tutorials while talking about raising three kids. Her show is called Child-Proof Lox."

I nodded. "Clever." I'd never been interested in

having children of my own, but Pippa had an eleven-month-old at home, so she had a stake in the ins and outs of raising kids.

"You think I'll be able to get her autograph?" Pippa asked.

"Probably."

"Oh. My. Gawd. I am wigging out!" I heard a woman shout. "It's Nora. Nora Black."

I turned at the sound of my name. Two women dressed in poofy, ankle-length prom dresses, one purple, the other orange, hurried in my direction.

Pippa grinned. "It seems Nellie Lox isn't the only one with fans here."

My Pinstabook channel, Scents and Scentsability, named for my shop, had a modest following, but it wouldn't be the first time I'd been recognized by homemade soap crafters while I'd been out and about.

"How are you?" the woman in purple asked. "It's been ages."

Okay. She acted as if she knew me. Probably not a fan.

The excited woman had a Princess Diana hairstyle, and I couldn't tell if it was a wig or her natural hair. She looked around. "Is Shawn here? I heard you two tied the knot."

Shawn Rafferty had been my high school sweetheart. Shortly after we'd started college, we'd gotten married. Five years after that, we'd divorced. We'd loved each other, but we'd wanted different things from life. Now, Shawn was the police chief in Garden Cove and married to a lovely woman who'd given him two handsome boys. And...he was my current boyfriend's boss.

"We're divorced," I told her, still trying to piece out who she was.

"I'm so sorry to hear that," Orange said sympathetically. Her hair was styled similarly to her friend's, and there was something about the two women that seemed familiar. Even so, I couldn't place them.

"Don't be. The divorce happened over twenty-five years ago." I laughed, feeling awkward at the reunion with two women who were practical strangers. Ugh. Strangers who had known Shawn and me when we were a "we." Had they gone to Garden Cove High? I'd graduated in a class of forty-eight total students, and while I'd known all their names at one point, I barely remembered a handful of them now.

I looked toward the dance floor where Gilly and Scott were rocking their moves, and I wished she was next to me. Her mind was a vault when it came to our teens. She remembered everything from those years.

Ezra draped his arm around me in a casual but meaningful way. "How do you two know Nora?" he asked the women.

I cast him a grateful glance.

"We were her sorority sisters," Purple exclaimed. "Kappa Nu!"

Orange cupped her ear, leaned in toward me, and added, "Kappa, who?"

I reluctantly responded with a weak, "Kappa, you, too." I pinched Ezra on the ribs when he chuckled, and it made him squirm.

"Fun," he said. "How long were you all sisters?"

Orange giggled. "Daffney and I have been sisters our whole lives."

A light bulb went off over my head. The Graves twins. Velma and Daffney. Even then, Velma dressed in orange and Daffney in purple. They had been in the same sorority rush class as me. I couldn't visualize what they'd looked like back in the '80s, but I did remember them getting asked about their names. It turned out their parents had been fans of Scooby-Doo the year the cartoon had started airing. Hence, they were Velma and Daffney. I guess they were lucky they hadn't been boys. One of them could've been Fred and the other Shaggy.

"It's so nice to see the two of you again, Velma." I tried not to look smug for merely remembering a name, but I couldn't help but feel like I'd scored points in the game of midlife. "I was only with the sorority for two semesters."

"Once a Kappa Nu, always a Kappa Nu," Daffney said.

"Do you all live around here? Or like us, just tourists?"

"We graduated from Button Falls," Velma gushed. She raised her hand as if shaking a pom-pom. "Go Vikings! We couldn't resist being first in line when we heard our old alma mater had been turned into a weekend mystery getaway."

Daffney smiled as she studied Ezra. "Nora, you haven't introduced us to your charming friend."

"Ezra Holden," I told them. "And Ezra, this is Velma and Daffney Graves. They're twins."

He looked mildly surprised. I wasn't sure if it was because of their names or because the two women were twins, but not identical.

"Fraternal twins," Velma said as if reading his mind. "My last name is Cormack now." She flashed her wedding rings, a wide platinum band with channel-set diamonds, and the engagement ring had to be at least three carats, also with channel-set diamonds around the band. "It'll be thirty years in May."

"Congratulations," I said. The guy was either well-to-do or in the poor house with the amount of money he must've spent on the rings. "Is he here with you?"

"Sisters' weekend," Daffney chimed in. "We couldn't resist an opportunity to reminisce. What a small world, running into you here. I can't wait to catch up. And it's lovely to meet you, Ezra."

"Any friend of Nora's," he said with a smile.

"Well, then let's be friends," Daffney said. She narrowed her gaze on the two of us as if suddenly finding us very interesting. "I would love to know more about how you guys met."

The music stopped as a commotion on the dance floor interrupted Daffney's prying into my personal life. *Yay, commotion.*

"Stay away from her," a guy with a light green letter jacket with white sleeves shouted. His mullet would have made Billy Ray Cyrus proud, and the back of his letter jacket had the name Cruise in big letters.

His anger was directed at the dude who wore the powder-blue tuxedo and Flock of Seagulls' hairstyle.

The brunette cheerleader tugged on the jock's arm. "Don't, Biff. Please. It's not worth it."

Their voices were loud and clear, amplified by the speakers. Ezra stepped forward to intervene, but I stopped him. "I'm pretty sure this is part of the weekend."

He frowned but hung back.

A Flock of Seagulls lunged for Biff, but a man in an ill-fitting brown suit stepped between them to intervene. Even with a bad gray wig, I recognized him as the man who'd almost knocked me over in the hall.

"Both of you, cool it," he said. "Unless you want to be in detention for the rest of the year."

"Sorry, Mr. Hughes," both guys said loudly and in unison.

Hughes waved to a man and a woman dressed like teachers. "Mr. Moore, could you escort Mr. Cruise out for some air?"

Mr. Moore turned out to be the guy who wore the beige slacks. He grabbed Cruise by the upper arm and dragged him out of the gym.

After, the principal turned to the woman channeling *Dynasty*. "Ms. Nelson, I need you to keep an eye on the other students," he cast a sweeping glance around at all of us in the gymnasium, "while I go have a talk with Mr. Bender, here." He marched the blue-tuxedo guy out of the gymnasium.

The names all made me smile. Moore, maybe for

Demi Moore, Cruise for Tom Cruise, and Bender, the Judd Nelson character in *The Breakfast Club*. Hughes, for John Hughes, of course, the writer and director of many movies that graced the eighties. Cheesy? Yes. Did I dig it? Absolutely.

"I'll never forgive you," the brunette cheerleader said to the blonde before rushing out of the gym.

"Mary, wait!" Blondie rushed after her friend.

"So much drama." Daffney clasped her hands. "I love it."

Ms. Nelson held up her hand as the chattering around the room grew to a dull roar. "Silence," she commanded. "You students stay in here while I step out for a moment." She pointed at the drinks table. "And nobody better spike the punch while I'm gone, or else you'll have Principal Hughes to deal with come Monday morning."

Gilly and Scott came off the dance floor and rejoined us. Gilly rubbed her hands together. "This is so freaking exciting."

I noticed Ezra was looking in the direction where Mr. Moore had escorted Cruise out the same door Ms. Nelson was now exiting.

Pippa moved in close to us. "I'm pretty sure all the actors have left the gym," Pippa said. "When will the mystery start?"

As if to answer her, a scream from the hallway

silenced us all quicker than Ms. Nelson had. Next, the gym door swung open, and the brunette cheerleader staggered inside. Her hands were red, and there were bloody prints on her white cheer sweater.

"Biff's dead," she cried out. "He's been...*murdered*!"

I glanced at Pippa and Gilly. "Race you to the crime scene."

CHAPTER
THREE

The body in the library was splayed face down between two bookshelves near the back of the room. The area around the dead guy had already been cordoned off with crime scene tape, and there was already yellow tape on the carpet around his body. I suspected the scene had been staged before the fight in the gym. Logistically, it made sense if they wanted to keep the murder mystery moving.

The victim had one arm above his head and one at his side. The hand above his head had a blue substance coating the fingers. His jacket was off, but the bloody mullet was unmistakable. This was Biff Cruise's corpse.

We could hear the music still blaring from the gym, and I couldn't help tapping my toe as "The Safety Dance" played in the background.

Ezra looked decidedly uncomfortable. "Why didn't they just turn off the music?" he asked me.

I smirked. "Don't try to apply your years of detective experience here. This is the eighties, baby." I adjusted the skirt on my dress. "Just go with it."

"Dude," Gilly said to him. "Take a chill pill. This is totally rad."

"Totally," I added. "Totally legit."

"Too legit to quit," Pippa added.

"That's so nineties." I blew a short raspberry. "Lame."

"Millennials." Gilly sucked her teeth as she tapped her six-inch-high bangs. "Totally bogus."

Pippa, who looked mildly insulted, adjusted her permed wig. "I've never seen two bigger dorks."

Gilly scoffed. "It's my birthday, and I can dork if I want to."

"What she said." Besides, I was having a lot more fun than I thought I would with this murder mystery weekend.

Scott chuckled. "I think it's bitchin'."

"Totally gnarly," Jordy added. Apparently, Ezra wasn't the only one to read the slang card in the welcome packet.

Gilly, Pippa, and I giggled.

The man who had played Principal Hughes was now in a blond feathered wig, and an oversized pale pink blazer with the sleeves pushed up to his elbows. He canvased the scene, making a display of jotting in his small notebook.

"I'm Detective Tubbs Crockett." He withdrew a badge from his pocket. "BFPD Homicide Unit. This is my crime scene. You're just visiting." He'd changed his voice to a different tone and made it raspier. If I hadn't been looking at him, I wouldn't have known he was the same guy playing the principal in the gym. Really, for an insufferable ass in an amateur role, he had some versatility.

"Very *Miami Vice*," Gilly whispered. "Didn't you have a crush on the star?"

"Hush," I said. I didn't need Ezra knowing that I had a poster of Don Johnson hanging up in my bedroom for the last two years of high school. "Besides, this guy is no Sonny Crockett."

"You certainly have a type," Pippa teased.

"Guys with badges and guns," Gilly poked.

"I get it," I told her, then pivoted my gaze between the two of them. "I'm going to trade you two in for new friends."

The Graves twins picked that moment to squeeze in next to us. Daffney brushed her shoulder against mine. "What happened?"

I pointed at Biff. "Dead body. Mystery on."

"Mega," Velma said. "How'd he die?"

"I think we're about to find out," Gilly interjected.

Detective Crockett pulled his beige linen pants up at the knees, exposing his loafers with no socks as he knelt next to the victim. As he examined the body, I wondered if he had been the "pizza face" or one of the jerks in the Drakkar Noir vision.

"He just touched the corpse," Ezra said, disgusted. "He should wait for crime scene techs to catalog and photograph everything before disturbing the remains."

"This isn't real," I reminded him.

He huffed his frustration. "Tell me about it."

"Nora, look. He's missing a shoe," Gilly whispered.

"Yep." The victim had on one white high top with green and black shoestrings. The other foot was covered in a white sock that had a similar blue substance to what was on his fingers. "What's the blue stuff on him?"

"It looks like pool cue chalk," Ezra mused.

"Are we sure he's alive?" Jordy asked. "That guy hasn't so much as twitched."

I saw a very subtle rise and fall of his chest. "He's alive," I replied.

"Quiet down." Detective Tubbs Crockett gave us

a stern glare. "Unless you want to get hauled down to the station for questioning."

"Didn't realize it was against the rules to talk," Ezra challenged him.

"You gotta know the rules to break the rules, preppy-boy," Crockett countered.

"Turn off your work brain," I said under my breath. I slipped my hand into his. "He's playing a role, is all."

Ezra shook his head. "I know. I just think if you're going to do something, you should do it right." He frowned, and with his new beard, managed to look grumpy and sexy all at the same time.

"Are you okay?"

"Fine," he said. He forced a smile. "I'm not sure my work brain has an off switch."

I could help with that. "Maybe later we can sneak away to our room."

His smile turned genuine. "This weekend is looking up."

Ms. Nelson, the "teacher" who had silenced us earlier, walked behind the crime scene tape carrying a stack of manilla envelopes.

She pushed her glasses up her nose and smiled. "Good evening, everyone, and Welcome to *School's Out for Murder*."

We all clapped, some more enthusiastically than others. And by some, I mean Daffney and Velma.

"I'm Demi Nelson, the music teacher here at Central High School, and I'll be your host for this weekend of misadventure."

We clapped again.

Her smile widened. "One of your fellow students, Biff Cruise, has been murdered. These packets contain the list of suspects, a medical examiner's report on the death, and background on the victim. There are other clues planted in different rooms in the school, except for the guest wing where you're staying, of course. Some of these rooms are locked-room puzzles, so you will need to figure out the clues to find the code to escape. And some you will need to find the code to enter. The locked rooms are monitored with surveillance cameras, so if you get in trouble, just yell for help, and we will provide extra clues to help get you out."

"Good to know," I whispered to Ezra. "No locked-room nookie."

He snickered and wrapped his arms around me from behind.

Ms. Nelson waved a hand. "Also, the kitchen area, other than the cafeteria line and anything marked *Staff Only,* is off-limits. You can interview suspects in the gymnasium at your leisure during the hours allotted on the schedule, but please be respectful of the suspects, witnesses, and your fellow sleuths by limiting the time of your interactions. And please put any clues you come across back where you found them so that everyone has a chance to find them." She gestured to Detective Crockett and the victim. "Can you discover who murdered Biff Cruise?" Her grin grew sly. "And can you stop the killer from striking again?"

"Does this mean there will be two murders?" Gilly whispered.

"Maybe," I whispered back.

A "shhhh" came from somewhere behind us.

Gilly and I made faces at each other then giggled.

"Everyone should have a partner. Either one you came with or one you have been assigned." Ms. Nelson held out the envelopes. "Each pair of sleuths gets a clue packet to share. There is a sheet in there for you to take notes, along with a list of suspects for you to investigate. After you get your clue packet, please wait in the hallway for us to clear the victim from the library. After, you will be allowed back into the library with full access to the crime scene to start your investigation."

The Graves sisters pushed past me and grabbed their packet first.

Ms. Nelson, unfazed by the twins' enthusiasm, continued. "There are sacked sandwiches, chips, apples, and drinks in the cafeteria lunch line if you get hungry. Just through the door at the back of the gym."

I smiled as Ezra nudged me.

"Breakfast will be served between six and nine tomorrow morning. Lunch will be from noon to two. During those times, the three locked rooms will be off-limits, but the unmonitored rooms will remain open for investigation."

She waited for a moment as if expecting questions. When none came, Ms. Nelson nodded. "Anything laminated needs to be returned with these envelopes after the mystery concludes. There are dry-erase pens in the packet for your use, and please don't use regular pens or permanent markers. Remember, you must leave the clues you find in the escape rooms. Staff will reset the scenes for each investigative team."

She raised a finger. "When you are ready to guess the killer, write down your answer and find me. I will log the time of your entry. The player who guesses the who, how, and why of the murder before anyone else will get to read the suspect summation and reveal the killer in front of everyone. They will also get a *School's Out for Murder* Super Sleuth badge and," she winked at us, "total bragging rights."

"I'm definitely getting the badge," Gilly said as Ms. Nelson finished passing out the information packets. "And the bragging rights."

"Nope," Pippa said. "That badge is all mine."

"I'm sorry to tell you both, but I will be walking out of this place, wearing that badge for all the world to see, and you will be calling me Super Sleuth from now on," I teased.

"Not happening," Gilly countered. "No way."

"Yes, way," I replied.

"Nope."

"Yep."

"Nuh-uh."

"Yuh-huh."

"Someone stop them," Pippa groaned. Then the three of us laughed.

"I can't believe you talked me into doing this," someone hissed from behind us. I looked back over my shoulder and saw Nellie Lox and the man she had been with near the punch table.

"This is ridiculous," the woman said. "You said this would be a romantic getaway without the kids."

Yikes. The murder mystery weekend was fun, but I wasn't sure it was a romance destination.

The guy said, "Come on, baby. Just give it a chance."

"I want to go back to the room," she huffed. "I can't believe you let them take my phone. I promised my fans I would document this as a No-Child weekend to show them that they don't have to stay home all the time to be good parents. Besides, we're paying the nanny a lot of overtime to take the children for the entire weekend. If I had my phone, I could write her salary off on taxes."

Gilly snickered. "I'm so glad we didn't have cellphones to document our high school shenanigans. Or share our every freaking moment on social media."

"You can say that again," I muttered.

"I really thought they'd let you keep your cellphone, Nellie," the guy said in a cajoling tone. "Can't we just this once do something for the two of us?"

"You're right, Harry." She put her arms around him. "Still, I'm sorry I won't be able to document our adventure. My Pinstabook fans would totally love this." She gestured as if captioning her next words. "Murder, mystery, no children, and eighties' makeup."

"Like that other Pinstabooker?" Harry asked.

"No," Nellie protested, "because I do it better."

He kissed her cheek. "Yes, you do."

I snorted as I took our packet. I didn't have to have a psychic vision to know that Harry had probably been well aware the weekend was a "no phones allowed" event.

Ezra chuckled as we left the library and moved out to the hall. He leaned down and pressed his lips to my ear. "These jeans are cutting off the circulation to my junk."

"Talk about romantic." I giggled. "You should try wearing the jeans we actually wore in the '80s. You had to lay down on the bed and use pliers or the hook end of a wire hanger to zip them up. And the men's jeans were so snug in the crotch it made their packages look like moose knuckles."

"Ouch," he said, automatically adjusting himself as men do whenever the idea of groin pain is mentioned.

I nodded. "And while I loved the eighties, I hope to never experience a camel toe ever again."

"Amen, sister," Gilly added. "Frankly, the way we strangled our ovaries and testicles, I'm surprised teen pregnancy even existed when we were in high school."

"I'd like to put that theory to the test." He gently tugged my earlobe between his teeth, sending a thrill of pleasure through me. "We could sneak off to the locker room," he said.

"I'm in," I told him. "As long as it doesn't have surveillance cameras."

"I'm really impressed by how they managed to turn an old school building into an event venue," Scott said.

"I'm still not sure why you guys would choose to solve a fake murder mystery. Don't you get enough murder and mayhem in Garden Cove?" Jordy asked, only slightly joking.

We'd recently solved a murder that had involved Gilly's ex-husband. Not for her ex, though. As far as either of us was concerned, Gio could've rotted in jail. But he and Gilly had kids together, and having their father in jail hadn't been good for Marco and Ari. On top of that, Pippa had inadvertently ended up in the killer's sights.

"Nope," Gilly replied. "Besides, it'll be nice being able to solve a murder, fake or not, before Nora. You know, since she can't use her smell-o-vision to sniff out the clues."

"And isn't that a nice change of pace," Pippa added.

"That I can't beat you guys to finding the murderer or that it's not real?" I asked.

The question garnered me a side look from my blonde bestie. "This is the first weekend Jordy and I have had away from the baby. I miss J.J. terribly, but

I'm also ready to screw my husband's brains out all over this school in-between crime-solving."

Jordy put his arm around Pippa's shoulder. "I'm good with that plan."

Pippa had never been a prude, but she'd also never been one to publicly talk about her personal stuff, especially not her sex life. I think having a baby had lowered her GAF, aka Give a Flip.

I circled my finger. "I think it's time to pair off so we can get a look at these clues."

"Agreed," Gilly said. She dragged Scott off closer to the gym doors. Pippa and Jordy walked about ten feet from us and opened their envelope outside of the school office.

Ezra took my hand. "I love your determination."

"I do like to win," I said.

"We have that in common."

There were two sets of doors to the library. The public one, and the one at the back that was marked "Staff Only." Biff Cruise, the dead guy, walked out of those doors. Ms. Nelson followed out behind him. They spoke for a moment, but their voices were hushed, and they were far enough away that I wouldn't have been able to hear them even if they had been speaking louder. Ms. Nelson looked upset for a moment, then her expression hardened before she went back inside the library.

Biff glanced in our direction. He gave us a half-smile and a wave as he headed past the library and through the "Staff Only" double doors.

Ezra shrugged as Biff disappeared behind the curtain, so to speak. "Well," he said. "It's time to put on our detective hats and find us a killer."

CHAPTER
FOUR

"You want to check out the library?" Ezra asked.

"No," I said. "Let's check out the chemistry room first."

"Why the chemistry room?"

Gilly, Scott, Pippa, and Jordy went into the library right away, along with all the other teams, but I'd stayed in the hall to examine the contents of the clue package first.

I lowered my voice so none of the other players would overhear me. "According to the medical examiner's report, the blue substance on the victim's fingers and sock was powdered copper sulfate."

"How is copper blue?"

"Copper sulfate is known as blue vitriol. It does look a lot like pool cue chalk when it's in powder form. It's used in pesticides, but it's not generally lethal unless you ingest it. Still, if he had the chemical on his hands and on his sock, I think it had to have come from the chemistry lab."

His expression was impressed. "How in the world do you know this?"

"I'd like to say it's because I remember my chemistry from college, but actually, it's because of that bird bath fountain you bought me for my birthday."

"I have no idea where this is going," he said with a wink. "But if you want to thank me again, I'm sure we can find a janitor's closet close by."

I gave a quick head shake and smiled. "Even with the circulating water, the fountain can get yucky. Bugs, mosquito larvae, algae, and so on."

"Oh." He made a face. "That sounds terrible."

"I love the fountain." Ezra had bought me a beautiful three-tier equinox fountain for my backyard because I'd happened to mention how much I'd admired one we saw on a country drive. If I hadn't already been in love with him, that would have done the trick. It was rare finding someone who listened to you when you talked.

"Besides, the fix was easy. I bought a liquid blue fountain treatment called Waterprep, put a few drops in, and it made the water crystal clear. Bonus, it's safe for birds and other animals when it's diluted and used as directed." I frowned. "Except for fish. Anyhow, I went down a whole rabbit hole on the internet learning about the stuff. It turns out the blue is from copper sulfate."

"Is that what killed the victim?"

I tapped the envelope. "Biff was hit on the back of the head and strangled."

"That's overkill."

I snorted. "Yep. Anyhow, whatever he was hit with wasn't found in the library. Nor was the cord or whatever the killer used to garrote Biff."

"How did the cheerleader end up with so much blood on her?"

"According to the witness statement," I sorted through the packet until I found the right one. "Mary Jane Masterson went into the library looking for Biff to break up with him, and she found him on the ground. She said she'd tried to turn him over, but when she saw all the blood, she left him where he was."

"That's when she figured out he was dead?" He rubbed the bridge of his nose. "Okay. So, the cheerleader was going to break up with Biff. Is that what the fight with the other guy was about?"

"The other guy being Brian Bender," I said.

"Brian and Mary Jane are from two different social cliques, and they've been secretly going out for the past two months. Biff caught them kissing behind the gym before the dance and confronted them on the dance floor."

"Wow, witnesses and suspects readily volunteering damaging information. I wish my job was that easy." He chuckled. "What happened with Mr. Moore when he took Biff out of the gym?"

"Mr. Moore is the science teacher. He says he told Biff to stay in the office and cool off, then he went to the teachers' lounge to get some coffee."

"He took a coffee break?"

"Apparently, he'd smelled alcohol on Biff and wanted to help sober up the star football player."

"Did the ME report include a blood-alcohol level for Biff the Stiff?"

I choked out a laugh. "Results inconclusive," I said.

"On blood alcohol levels?" Ezra frowned. "But you said that results for the blue gunk were part of the report."

I quirked a brow. "Suspicious."

He nodded. "Convoluted."

I grinned. "In the best way." I had to admit, I was really starting to get into the mystery.

"You know, if this were a real murder, I'd start with the crime scene."

"Yes," I agreed. "But it's not. We need to get a head start on the escape rooms."

"You really want to beat Pippa and Gilly, don't you?"

"I really, really do." Gilly had thrown down the gauntlet, all in good fun, that I wouldn't be able to sleuth my way out of a paper bag without my psychic aroma-mojo. I planned to prove her wrong. I tapped the packet. "Copper sulfate might not be the murder weapon, but it's a pretty big clue."

Ezra took my hand, lacing his fingers with mine. "Let's go before some other bird bath aficionado figures it out."

The school map showed that the building was shaped like a squared-off number eight with a fat middle. Eight hallways made up the loops. The center halls housed the gymnasium that doubled as a cafeteria. The kitchen was located on the backside of the gym, and across the hall was the office along with the library. The west-facing hallways were staff only. The east hallways were comprised of the guest quarters and the classrooms.

But we didn't need the map to navigate. We followed the posted signs to the classrooms.

"How did Biff have time to leave the front office, go all the way to the chemistry lab to get blue gunk on him, and end up murdered in the library?"

"According to the witness statements in the clue packet, forty-five minutes passed between Biff being escorted from the dance to Mary Jane Masterson, the brunette cheerleader, finding him."

"So, the five minutes that passed before the scream was an accelerated timeline."

"Looks like it."

Only one fluorescent light illuminated the hall. It flickered ominously, clicking and popping like a bug zapper.

The noisy bulbs flickered again, reminding me of every horror movie that had ever taken place in a high school. "Wow. They've upped the creep factor by a hundred."

Ezra put his arm around me. "You afraid of Freddy Krueger?"

"Uh...*yeah*. And Jason. And Michael. And the *Children of the Corn*."

"I won't let the boogeyman hurt you." He pointed to the second room on the left. Chemistry Lab was written on a door plaque. "We found it."

"Looks like the escape rooms are all together." On the other side of the chemistry lab was a door labeled History. Across the hall, I saw the Math and English classrooms. Those had keypads on their doors. "Hmm." I tapped my chin. "We'll probably have to find the right combinations to get inside."

"If they made it too easy, it would be more a mystery evening than a weekend, I suppose," Ezra said.

Neither the Chemistry Lab nor the History room had keypads, and the lab door opened easily. Moonlight filtered in through the high windows, making everything in the dark room appear in silhouette. The door closed behind us. A beep sounded as it shut, and a red light began to blink.

Even though I knew the mystery was fake, my pulse picked up the pace.

Ezra tried the handle. "We're definitely locked in," he said. "There's a keypad on the back of the door with nine numbers and the letters A, B, and C."

"If the solution is math, we're going to be stuck in here for a very long time."

"I'll handle the math problems," said Ezra. "You get everything else."

"Deal," I said. "Let's get the lights turned on," I told Ezra. I gestured to the right. "I'll take this side. You take the other side."

"We make a great team." He tilted my head back

and dipped his lips to mine with a gentle press. Automatically, I went up on my toes to deepen the kiss. He tugged me closer, his hand cupping the back of my neck. As he eased back, he brushed my cheek with his fingers, sending a warm ache through me. "You're beautiful. How did I get so lucky?"

My breathing quickened along with the beating of my heart. A flashing red light in the corner of the room diverted my attention. "Oh, crap. We're being monitored. Possibly recorded."

Ezra smiled as he let go of me. "I forgot about that."

"No *Fast Times at Murder High* pornos will be made today," I said to whoever was in control on the other side of the camera.

"Noted. By the way, we don't record guests," a guy's voice said over the intercom. "But I can see everything that happens in the room." He sounded amused. "Welcome to Chemistry Chaos. You have twenty minutes to discover the clues and make your escape.

"What happens if we don't make it?" Ezra asked.

"You'll have to leave and try again later. This allows every team the same amount of time in each locked room."

I shrugged. "That makes sense."

"Do you guys want a hint?" the voice asked. "It will cost you five minutes of time."

"Nope," I answered. "We got this."

"Righteous," the guy said. "I'm here if you need me. Just wave your hand if I don't respond right away. I'm in charge of all the escape rooms, so the waving will alert me if I get busy."

I gave the camera a thumbs up. "Got it." I patted Ezra's chest. "Let's get the lights turned on."

We searched the walls but couldn't find the light switches. After a few minutes, our eyes adjusted to the low-level light enough to see there were six rectangular workstations with drawers and an instructor's workstation at the front of the class.

I started with the instructor's area and opened drawers. The first drawer on the top row was locked, but the rest weren't. When I slid open the fourth drawer, I yelled, "Bingo!"

Ezra walked over. "What did you find?"

"A flashlight," I told him. I clicked the button on the side. No light came on. "Fantabulous. It doesn't work." The end was loose, so I unscrewed it. It was empty. "It doesn't have batteries."

"Oh," Ezra exclaimed. "I found two C batteries in the first desk, top drawer."

We returned to the first student desk, and Ezra

opened the drawer. I held up the flashlight's open end.

"Which side goes down? Plus or minus?" he asked.

"Let's go nipple down, and if that doesn't work, we'll turn them around."

"That's what he said," Ezra joked.

I snorted a laugh. "You've been hanging around Gilly too much."

"Your fault," he countered with a smirk. He dropped the batteries inside the tube. "Here goes nothing."

I screwed the bottom back on the flashlight. The light came on, and I let out a triumphant, "Yes!" Then I noticed the purplish color of the beam. "Is this a black light?"

"UV light."

"Let's see what it picks up." We walked around the room, running the light over every science poster, the bookshelves, the windows... A glow of blue showed up on the third window. "Up there," I said. I shone the light over the window. "It's the numbers four, three, and one. Maybe those are for the keypad on the door."

I returned to the door and punched the numbers in. The light stayed red. I added the A, then tried again with the B, and finally with the C. The light never changed.

"Let's keep looking for more clues," Ezra said. I heard the excitement in his voice.

"Having fun, huh?"

He scratched his beard and chuckled. "Maybe."

I shined the light at him, and my eyes widened when his facial hair glowed in patches. "Hold on," I said. "Let me see your hands."

He held them out. Two of his fingers showed the substance. "What is it?"

"What have you touched since you've been in here?"

"Just the workstations." He shook his head. "But not all of them."

I ran the light around each of the stations, one at a time. The one nearest the windows in the second row had a blob of blue across the top with a smear where he must've touched it. "There," I told him.

"I walked past that one but didn't get a chance to go through it before you found the flashlight," Ezra said.

"Hmmm." I opened all the drawers. In glowing letters, the word *Find* was written in the top left drawer, the middle drawer had the word *The* in it, and the last drawer had the word *Key*. We opened the rest of the drawers, and other than smudgy prints, they were empty. "Well, poop."

"Ten minutes," the guy said over the intercom. "You have ten more minutes left to discover the clues and find a way out."

"Thanks," I said loudly.

"Do you want a hint?"

"And lose five of our ten minutes? No, thank you." Besides, my pride wouldn't allow me to take the hint. "We're going to figure this out."

"Good luck," the voice said.

"Four, three, one," I said to Ezra. "It has to mean something."

"This is the fourth station," Ezra said. "Maybe it has something to do with the drawer counts."

"Oh. Like the third row of drawers, first drawer in that row." I frowned when we pulled it open. "It's just as empty as the first time we looked inside. We've looked through all the drawers. Nothing."

"But we didn't look under them," Ezra said. He pointed up to a poster that was under the window where we'd found the numbers. "Everything Under the Sun."

"Seems a little in your face, but I'll take it." I loved that Ezra let me check under the drawer, even though I knew he was itching to see if he was right.

When I produced a small metal key, he gave a

fist pump of triumph. I grinned so hard my cheeks hurt. "There's a locked drawer in the teacher's station."

He rubbed his hands together. "Well, let's see if it fits."

The key opened the drawer, and cripes if my heart wasn't pounding as if I were being chased by Duran Duran in the *Hungry Like the Wolf* video. "There's a note and a grade book." I shined the UV light on the note. The white of the page was candescent. "You read it," I said. I didn't want to admit that even with surgery to correct my vision, I still had trouble with my near vision in low light.

Ezra plucked it from the drawer for a closer look.

"Mr. Moore, I know what you did, and unless you want everyone finding out, you'll change my grade from a D to a B. It's signed B.C. It has to be Biff Cruise, right?" Ezra nodded. "Isn't Mr. Moore the guy who took Biff to the office? The last person to see the victim alive?"

"I think so." I steepled my fingers. "The plot thickens." A familiar sweet herbal scent wafted from the note. "Do you smell that?"

"I'm really disappointed with your attitude," a woman says. Her face is unrecognizable, but she has straight brown hair with the front pulled up and back in a smooth bump on the top of her head. She's wearing a

blue cardigan and tapping her foot. "*You're better than what you show people. And you have a lot of talent. I hate to see it wasted.*"

"*Sorry,*" *a guy says. He's wearing a blue and gold sweatshirt, high tops, and jeans.* "*I'll apologize.*"

The woman sounds pleased as she nods. "*Good. If you want, I can help you. You're getting a D in my class right now. Some extra tutoring before and after school will pull that grade right up.*"

A noise outside the room startles them. The guy stands up and says, "*Thanks, Mrs. P.*"

"What did you see?" Ezra asked in a hushed voice.

"A super-uninteresting meeting between a student and a teacher named Mrs. P. I think he might've been either the geek or one of the bullies from my earlier vision. The teacher was definitely the same."

Ezra glanced up at the monitor as a reminder we were being watched. It's not like the guy would understand anything we were talking about, but still, we both turned so our backs were to the camera. Ezra lowered his voice and said, "Maybe you're picking up on stuff from when the school was still active. Some of the props can be leftover items."

I whispered my response. "Maybe. But this scent was on the note." I shook it off. "You know what.

Never mind. No one is dying, getting hurt, or anything else bad, so we're going to let it go. Besides, it doesn't have anything to do with the current mystery, and I'm not going to let it stop me from whooping Gilly and Pippa's butts."

"That's the spirit." Ezra patted me on the back.

"Five minutes," the guy said over the speakers.

"Crap." Ezra shoved the note back in the drawer. "Where's the door code?"

An idea struck me. "The grade book." I set it on the desktop and opened it up. "Just as I thought. There's a list of student names in here, including our four students from tonight. Biff, Brian, Mary Jane, and Leah Standish, the blonde cheerleader."

"How do we get the code from that? There's twenty-five names on the roster."

I nodded and began counting. "Look at the grades. There's five As, seven Bs, and seven Cs." I ignored the Ds and Fs since those letters weren't on the keypad.

Ezra went over to the electronic lock and punched in 5A7B7C. The red light turned green, there was a slight whirring sound, and the door opened.

"Yes!" I high-fived my guy. "We killed it."

"Nice job, folks," the disembodied voice said. "You managed Chemistry Chaos in sixteen minutes and forty-one seconds. I need your room number so I can mark your time."

"We're in room five." I gave the camera a final salute. "Thank you, Man-Behind-the-Curtain."

"Where to next?" Ezra asked as we exited the room.

"I think we need to interview Mr. Moore. He has some 'splainin' to do."

CHAPTER
FIVE

The suspects-slash-witnesses had all conveniently congregated in the gym as per the schedule. They stood a few feet away from each other as various guests asked them questions. Gilly and Scott were talking to Ms. Nelson. The young married couple were chatting up Brian Bender, Velma and Daffney had Mr. Moore cornered, and two other teams were talking to the cheerleaders. Pippa and Jordy weren't in the gym.

Ezra and I grabbed our sack dinners from the cafeteria line in the kitchen, which consisted of ham and cheese sandwiches, barbecue or plain chips, apples, a granola bar, and our choice of soda, milk, or water. I was a little tired, so I took a Diet Coke for the caffeine.

We sat on the bleachers and ate while we waited our turn to interview Mr. Moore.

"I've got bleacher butt," I complained. It had been about half an hour, and we weren't any closer to interrogating the science teacher.

"The twins sure are taking their time with our suspect," Ezra said. He jabbed my granola bar with his finger. "You going to eat that?"

"We're definitely having you tested for a tapeworm," I kidded. "But yes. You can have the granola bar. You can have my chips, too, if you want them."

His eyes crinkled at the corners when he smiled. "You really do love me."

"I really do." I gave him a quick kiss and brushed breadcrumbs from his beard. "Not sure I love the facial hair, but definitely the man it's attached to." I watched as the single Graves sister reached out and touched Mr. Moore's hand as she laughed at something he said. "Cripes. How long is Daffney going to monopolize Mr. Moore?" I complained.

"Come on," Ezra said. "Let's go check out the library. We can't talk to Moore with this many people around, anyhow. Not without giving up our advantage. We're the only ones who know he was being blackmailed by the victim, and I'd like to keep it that way for now."

I smirked. "Now, I'm the one impressed with your competitiveness."

"I was quite the athlete in high school," he said with a grin. "You know, before…" He made a round gesture at his belly.

"Before you swallowed a basketball?" I snickered. "Kidding." I squeezed his hand. "You're still quite the athlete."

Ezra had gotten his high school girlfriend pregnant when they were both sixteen years old. They'd gotten married, three years later divorced, but he'd done his best as a young man to be a good father. His son Mason was eighteen now and in college. They had a close relationship, thanks to family therapy. And if the young man was any indication of Ezra's measure, I'd say my guy was top-notch when it came to the dad stuff. I knew that wasn't always the case. My godchildren, Gilly's twins Marco and Ari, had turned out terrific, and they'd had a terrible father. So, the two things didn't always go hand in hand.

Still, I often marveled at the number of obstacles Ezra had overcome to become the man he was now. At thirty-four, he was the detective supervisor over special crimes for the Garden Cove Police Department.

"The library's a good idea," I told Ezra. "Let's do it."

He arched a brow. "And the library is not a locked room…"

I flushed. "I like where you're going with this, but first we'll examine the crime scene, then we can go hit the stacks."

"Kappa Nuuuu!" Daffney crooned as she marched in our direction.

"Oh no," I grumbled.

"Don't you mean, oh nuuuu." Ezra laughed.

"Hush," I said on a snort.

"You've got on sneakers," he said covertly. "We could make a break for it."

"Too late," I hissed. "I made eye contact."

"Hi, Daffney," Ezra said, a smile in his voice and a charming twinkle in his eye.

Daffney giggled. "Hello, Ezra." She gave him a wink. "Nora, where have you been? Your friend Jerry…Joy…Jill…"

"Gilly," I finished for her.

"Yes, her. She was looking for you earlier."

I looked over to where Gilly was conversing with Ms. Nelson. Her hands were animated with excitement as Scott watched her with complete adoration.

I shrugged. "Doesn't seem like she wants me now."

Daffney bounced on the tips of her pointy-toed pumps. "Uhm, can I talk to you...in private?"

"About?"

She glanced nervously at Ezra. She looked as if she was going to say something, but then her attention shifted to her sister Velma, who had started walking in our direction. Daffney shook her head. "Later, okay? Not now."

Ominous. "Okay. The mystery shuts down at eleven tonight."

Daffney forced a cheerful smile. "No hurry," she said quickly. "Tomorrow is fine. "

I frowned as she turned to intercept her sister.

"I think that's our cue to go." I grabbed Ezra's arm and took the opportunity to vamoose.

"Good idea," he said. I could tell by his expression he was as curious about Daffney's request as I was. "To the library, Sherlock?" he asked.

"Indeed, Watson," I replied.

Now that the crime scene was vacant, I took the time to appreciate the details that made it look like a high school library. All the shelves were filled with books. The yellow tape was still on the ground in the shape of a prone body, one arm up, one at the side, just like the pose Biff had been in earlier. There was a small dark spot inside the head area, presumably from the head wound.

"Heads bleed a lot more than that," I said. I'd taken a hit to the scalp last year while exposing a killer, so I knew from personal experience that even a minor cut could turn into a blood bath.

"They sure do," Ezra replied.

"But the cheerleader had a lot of blood on her uniform and hands."

"True," he agreed. "But like you said before, this isn't real. Which means they probably used fake blood to gore the cheerleader up so that she made the biggest impact when she ran into the gym. I don't think we can factor the lack of blood at the scene into our investigation."

"You're right." Still, it bothered me. It was like the time my goddaughter Ari had made me watch *Sharknado* with her. I could suspend my disbelief about flying sharks attacking the world, but I couldn't get past the hero dumping gasoline into a pool and making it explode by throwing a match at it.

"It just wouldn't happen," I'd told Ari.

She'd snarfed, "Out of everything going on in this movie, that's the thing you can't believe?"

She'd been right. The movie had been ridiculously unbelievable, but... "It just seems like the amount of blood from a head wound is something they could have researched better." Which is how I'd felt about the exploding pool.

"Nora, come look," Ezra said as he walked between two of the book stacks near the back of the library. "They have five different sets of encyclopedias on these shelves."

"Makes sense," I said as I joined him. "No one uses them anymore, and they fill up a lot of empty space." My mother had two sets on her bookshelves. After she died, I'd boxed them up and donated the lot to a children's charity.

Ezra grabbed me roughly enough for me to gasp, then stole my breath with a toe-curling kiss. I let the clue packet drop to the floor and wrapped my arms around him, enjoying the press of his body against mine. The scruff of his beard grazed my skin, and at the moment, I didn't care that my face was going to look like I'd recently had a chemical peel. I grasped his butt and felt giddy as he softly moaned against my mouth.

When he eased from the kiss, he said, "Damn, woman," in a way that made me melt.

I reached between us and rubbed my hand over the front of his jeans. He was rock hard. I smiled. "Is this what you wanted to show me?"

"Well, it certainly wasn't the encyclopedias." He kissed me again as his fingers slid down my sides to the hem of my skirt. It was tight enough that it wasn't coming up easily. Ezra chuckled. "Like trying to get into Fort Knox."

"The zipper," I muttered as I undid the top button on his jeans.

"Right," he said. "On the side."

The back door opening and closing, followed by voices, froze us in place.

"Well, crap," Ezra mouthed. He buttoned his jeans back up and straightened my dress and hair.

"We can't talk now," a woman whispered, making it hard to identify who she might be. "I just wanted to hold you for a moment."

"He's on to us."

"You're being paranoid," the woman told him.

"You didn't see the way he talked to me earlier. He knows."

"I'm so afraid of him," the woman said softly. "If he knows, he's going to kill me."

"I can't stand the way he touches you, the way he looks at you," the guy murmured.

"I have to play along with him. He has to think I...that I still love him."

The guy's voice became thick and low. "You're mine."

"Not yet. But soon, my love, I'll be all yours," the woman assured him. "But for now, we dream, so we don't have to be apart for so long."

"If we're in each other's dreams," the guy responded, "we can be together all the time."

Their words sounded familiar, as if I'd heard them before. Before I could figure it out, the bookshelf in front of us shook and then there were kissy, slurpy noises.

I blinked rapidly at Ezra. "Oh, my gawd," I mouthed.

His eyes were wide, and I could tell he wanted to bolt. Neither of us wanted to sit quietly while people had sex a few feet from us. If it came down to it, I was completely prepared to make a lot of noise to give them a heads up that they had an audience.

My nose twitched as a familiar aroma wafted on the air. It was that damn Drakkar Noir scent again. Ezra raised his brow in a question.

Before I could answer, the citrus and pine with notes of leather and moss took me over.

A woman with dark blonde hair sits on a brown leather loveseat. I see a lamp, Tiffany-style shade, near her, and there is a bookshelf behind. All the titles are a jumble of nonsensical letters that are unreadable. She holds a child, not more than five or six years old, if size is an indication. The child wore jeans and a green t-shirt and I couldn't tell by the clothes which seemed unisex, if it was a boy or a girl.

The woman spritzes the air and the child with a fine mist. "This always reminds me of your father," she says as she stands up and twirls the child in her arms as "What's Love Got to Do With It" comes on the stereo. "He's coming back." The woman, her words slightly slurred, sounds high or drunk. "You just wait. If you're good. He'll come back."

Ezra tightened his arms around me. "You okay?"

"Yeah." I focused my eyes. "Are they gone?"

"The guy heard a beep and said he had to go, and the woman followed him out."

"Did you see who it was?"

Ezra shook his head. "I was too busy trying to keep you upright. You really zoned out on that one. What did you see?"

"It... I'm not sure. It was a nice memory, but it didn't feel...happy."

"What makes you say that?"

"It was a mom with her kid, or at least I think so. But I'm pretty sure the memory was the kid's."

"Why?"

"The books," I said. "There wasn't a single title that made any sense."

"Was it in this library?"

I shook my head again, unable to shake the

feeling of unease. "It isn't a memory I can do anything about."

Ezra smiled. "So, who do you think it was? Making out against the bookshelf, I mean."

"With that cologne, I'm going with Detective Tubbs Crockett," I said. "He smelled like he'd bathed in it earlier. Though, he doesn't seem like the secret lover type."

Ezra's expression darkened. "There is something about that guy. I just can't shake the feeling that I've seen him somewhere."

"Are you sure that's not just two weeks of living with bad guys talking?"

He rubbed his beard. "Maybe. When all you look for are zebras, all you see is zebras, even in a field of horses."

I laughed. "Eloquently put."

"I am good with words," he said.

"Yeah, you are." I gave him a quick kiss. "Even though the scent points to Tubbs Crockett, I don't think the memory is his."

"How come?"

"Tina Turner singing 'What's Love Got to Do With It' was playing in the memory. It came out in the early nineteen eighties. Crocket is older than me by a few years. In other words, he can't be the small child that was being spritzed by his mom. I graduated in eighty-six, so he would've been out of high school by then." I was looking at the rows of encyclopedias as I tried to reconcile my vision with the scent. That's when I noticed... "Hey, there's a green one nestled in the maroon collection." I pulled the book from the shelf. It was for the letter T.

"All five stacks have books out of place," Ezra said. "Here's a blue one in the green set." It was an M. A maroon H was in the brown set, and a brown A was in the blue set.

I grinned. "It spells Math," I told him. "And look." The back of every book had a number taped on it. "One, Six, Nine, Five." I fetched the clue packet from the floor and took out the note sheet and wrote the combination down.

"Let's put them back," I said. "Before someone sees them and figures out the clue because of us."

"We will get bragging rights," Ezra told me as we quickly put the encyclopedias back on the shelves.

"Damn straight. And the super sleuth badge."

CHAPTER SIX

We decided to try the gym one more time to see if we could talk to Moore before going to the Math classroom. Plus, we wanted to throw off anyone who might trace our steps back to where we found the door combination. As we walked through the auditorium, I could barely contain my excitement. Eighties rock and pop music continued to pour out of the speakers at a level that was just above background noise. The Go-Go's "We Got the Beat" was currently in the rotation.

"Hey," Gilly said, coming up behind me. "Where have you two been hiding?"

"Nowhere."

"Have you found anything...interesting?" she asked.

I scanned the gymnasium and changed the

subject so I wouldn't give away the clues we'd found. I couldn't lie to my BFF, but I could avoid with the best of them. "Have you seen Pippa and Jordy?"

"Earlier in the library." Gilly eyed me suspiciously. "Wait a minute. You're avoiding the question. You know something, don't you? You know you can't fib around me, Nora. I can read you like a book."

Her assessment hit close to home as far as the new clue went. I made a key-to-lock motion on my lips then threw away the key. "You'll get nothing outta me."

She turned her mom-gaze on me, but I'm immune to the parental death stare. When I wouldn't say more, she let out a frustrated noise. "Come on. It's my birthday. Just a hint. We've been over the crime scene, the packet, and interviewed everyone. Other than the fact that bohunk Biff was a jealous butthead, I've got bupkis."

Crap. Playing the BFF Birthday card was way more effective than the mom gaze. I glanced at Ezra apologetically. "When you get to the chemistry room, check the drawers." I pointed toward the ceiling. "And look up."

Ezra groaned as Gilly threw her arms around me

and noisily kissed my cheek. "This doesn't mean you get credit if I win," she said.

"Duly noted," I told her. "I wouldn't expect anything less than a full denial that I gave you any help."

She happily scampered off in Scott's direction.

Ezra raised both brows at me.

"It's her birthday," I said in my defense. "Consider it my gift."

He chuckled as he slung an arm over my shoulders. "No more gifts."

"None." I crossed my heart. "Hey, it looks like the science teacher is on his own. Let's nab him while we can."

Mr. Ren Moore, according to the historical background of the character, had been a teacher for fifteen years at Central High School. He was married with two elementary-aged children, and he was well-liked by students and staff. Only Ezra and I knew that one student hadn't liked the man.

"Mr. Moore, can we have a private word?" I asked.

He pointed up and twirled his finger. "That's what the music is for. It's not so loud we can't talk, but loud enough that our conversation won't carry."

I looked around and tried to hear the conversation the young couple was having with the cheerleader Leah Standish, and realized I couldn't make out anything they were saying.

I nodded. "Impressive."

His smile was beaming, and it gave his face a more youthful appearance. I guessed him to be his early to mid-forties. "What can I do for you?"

I glanced at Ezra.

He gestured for me to go ahead.

Since he wasn't a real suspect for a real murder, I decided to go for the direct approach. "How long has Biff Cruise been blackmailing you?"

Moore managed to appear shocked. "What makes you think he was blackmailing me?"

"Oh, I don't know. An incriminating letter in the locked drawer of your desk, perhaps?" I pointed an accusing finger at him. "What did he have on you, sir? And was it enough for you to kill him to hide your secret?"

He shook his head. "It's true Biff was blackmailing me. Or at least trying to, but I wasn't going to change his grade to keep my secret." A slight smile tugged at the corner of his lips. "As to what he had on me, that's for me to know and you to find out."

"Are you denying you killed him?"

"I was getting coffee in the breakroom," he said evasively.

"For forty-five minutes?" Ezra interjected.

Moore crossed his arms over his chest. "The pot is a slow percolator."

"Can anyone vouch for your whereabouts?" I asked.

"When I dropped Biff off in the office, I didn't know I was going to need an alibi," he said smoothly. "Do you meddling kids have any more questions?"

"Nope. Thanks for your time."

He spread his hands. "I'll be here all night."

The other actors-slash-characters were all engaged with other guests...except Tubbs Crockett, who was dressed in the dark brown wig and ill-fitting suit. So, he was now Mr. Hughes, the principal. "Do you want to talk to that guy?" I asked Ezra.

"I don't," Ezra admitted. "There's something familiar about the man. I know him from somewhere, but I can't put my finger on it."

"Like in an official capacity?"

"Maybe," he said. He jammed his hands in his pockets. "I remember every person I ever booked, so I don't think he's someone I arrested. Still, he doesn't feel like a witness or another cop." He shook his head. "It'll come to me. Until then, I'd like to keep my distance."

"That's good by me." Hughes-Crockett's cologne

kept sending me down psychic memory lane. I was happy to avoid another run-in. "So, the Math room?"

"Let's do it," Ezra said. "If Gilly or Pippa comes around, we wait until they are scarce before we punch in the code."

I nodded. "Yep. Totally."

He kept his gaze on me.

"I swear," I said.

"Until Gilly guilts you again."

I grinned. "Exactly."

We waited for the Graves sisters to go inside the History classroom. I didn't see Gilly or Scott, so I assumed they were trying to figure out Chemistry Chaos.

I punched in the code on the Math room door: 1695. The light on the keypad turned green, and the lock clicked.

Ezra grabbed the handle and pulled the door open. His smile was victorious.

"We're awesome," I said as we rushed inside.

"You'll get no argument from me." He let the door close behind us.

I tugged on a front belt loop on his jeans. "Alone again. Whatever shall we do with our time?"

Ezra rested his arms on my shoulders. "I'm sure something will come up."

Suddenly, the ceiling lights flared to life, putting the kibosh on sexy time.

"Welcome to Math Madness, folks," the guy over the intercom said.

That's when we noticed there was another keypad on the interior of the door. Ugh. It didn't occur to me that there would be a keypad on the inside, too. But I should've remembered it was an escape room before attacking Ezra.

"You have twenty minutes to find the clues and escape," the guy said. "If you need a hint, just say help. Every hint will cost you five minutes."

"Thank you, cockblocking Man-Behind-The-Curtain."

"Here's a free hint," the guy added with a chuckle. "If you want privacy, you should've gone to a hotel."

I rolled my eyes at the camera then turned my gaze to Ezra. "At least the lights are on this time. Should make stuff easier to find."

He pointed to a mash-up of equations using numbers and letters that covered the entire surface of the whiteboard at the front of the class. "I'm not sure easy is the right word."

"Nope," I agreed. "Numbers are hard."

The room had a teacher's desk, twenty student desks, some cabinets and counter space on the wall with the door. Outside the windows was a view of a lighted courtyard.

The slightly sour scent of dry erase markers made my tummy feel icky. Again, it was a bit anachronistic since I was sure that most the schools in the '80s had chalkboards, but I imagined the whiteboards were easier to maintain.

"Are you okay?" Ezra asked.

"Absolutely. The smell of dry-erase markers upsets my stomach."

"Visions?" he asked quietly.

"No more bullies versus geeks, Mrs. P and the jock, or the boy and his mom, thankfully." I wasn't worried. "Honestly, I just need to stay away from Hughes-Crockett. His cologne is really doing a number on me tonight."

Ezra started pulling out drawers, checking them inside, outside, top, and bottom. "There's definitely something about him that rubs me the wrong way."

I would have liked to rub my boyfriend the right way, but, alas, there was an audience. "He seems harmless enough, though, right?"

"You mean other than when he knocked you over then flipped us off?" He found a lockbox with a six-number combination in the bottom right drawer. "Yes!"

"This'll be easy." I joined him on the other side of the desk. "There's only a gazillion combinations. Nooo problem." I spun the first dial around. "Strange."

"What?"

"These turn dials only have numbers one through six. There's no zero, and it doesn't go up to nine like most combo locks."

Ezra spun it around toward him. "Good news. That makes it a million or so combos less."

I stared with anxiety at the whiteboard. "If the answer is in that mess, we're screwed. We might as well tell The Wiz behind the camera to let us out, so we can ease on down the road, so to speak."

"You're the one who told me the answers are usually obvious, so I think most of the stuff on the board is a red herring. You go through the desks. I'll check the shelves. Between the two of us, we'll find the right code to unlock the door."

"I don't suppose there was a grade book in the desk?"

Ezra gave me a hug. "Nope. Not this time."

I didn't see anything inside the students' desks,

but as I ran my fingers across the smooth top of one of them, I felt a scratched-in groove about an inch long on the corner. I peered closer and could make out a notched end. "Hey, there's an arrow on this desk," I told Ezra. There were some initials next to it. "Next to it says BB + MJ."

"Brian Bender plus Mary Jane." Ezra joined me at the desk. "That tracks with the jealousy tantrum in the gym."

"Fifteen minutes," the guy over the intercom said.

"We better get going." Ezra leaned down and nodded. "The arrow is pointing to the right." He moved to the next one. He practically skipped around when he found another arrow. "It's pointing toward the desk behind it."

My adrenaline ramped up a notch as we went from one desk to another, following the arrows to their conclusion: the last window at the back of the room.

I groaned. "I'm going to start looking at windows first from now on." There wasn't anything on the window that I could see. "I don't get it."

"What's that on the ledge?" Ezra asked.

"I can't believe I missed it." On the wooden ledge, someone had used a knife to carve the word *blow*. So, I blew. As the window fogged from my breath, the number 3 was revealed on the pane in the condensation. I did a quick count. I spoke rapidly. "There are six windows. We need six numbers for the combination. We need to blow on all of them."

We laughed together like giddy teenagers as we proceeded to reveal all the numbers on the panes. It was nice seeing Ezra relaxing and having genuine fun.

We raced from one window to the next, and I got to the final one before Ezra. "Dibs," I called.

He wrapped his arms around me from behind. "It's all yours."

My breath revealed a number 4. I noticed the latch wasn't turned the same way as the others. Was that part of the clue? Did it indicate order? I tugged it, and the window opened. That's when I detected the skunky scent of marijuana mixed with the tart-sweet smell of cherries.

"I'll do it," a guy says. "For you, I'll do anything." His face is a fuzzy mess, but he has short brown hair, and he's wearing jeans and a gray sweatshirt. He takes a tug on a joint. "I wasn't ready before, but I am now."

A woman, a blonde, puts her hand on his arm. She's wearing jeans and a red sweater. "Are you sure? I...we could just stop. Like we did before. He never has to find out. No one does."

"There's nothing keeping us apart now. You can't get in trouble anymore. He's the only thing standing between us." He stubs the joint onto the latch and brushes the debris out the window before putting the roach in his pocket. *"I'll do it. I'll take care of him this weekend."*

"It has to look like an accident," she says.

"Don't worry, Winnie." He kisses her. *"By the time the opening weekend is over, he'll be dead, and no one will even look in your direction."*

"Oh." My eyes widened as I transitioned from memory to the present time. This wasn't some distant plan from prior decades. The room had been this room. The way it looked *now*.

"You look like you saw a ghost," Ezra said.

"Not a ghost," I told him, still shaken from the memory. "But there might be a murder if we don't stop it."

Ezra's eyes widened. He glanced toward the camera then tugged me into an embrace. In my ear, he whispered, "Let's take this conversation somewhere that doesn't have eyes and ears."

CHAPTER
SEVEN

"I'm sorry, what?" Gilly asked. We'd grabbed her and Scott when they'd exited Chemistry Chaos and dragged them to our guest room.

Scott, who had gotten a front-row seat to my smell-o-rama show a few months back, leaned against the dressing table. He crossed his arms. "Are you sure there's going to be a murder this weekend? I mean, maybe they were just acting out a scenario for a future mystery."

Ezra assessed the doctor and nodded. "That's a good thought."

I frowned as a tension headache began to take hold. I massaged the space above the bridge of my nose. "I don't think so. My visions are triggered by scents, but only if the emotional memories attached to them are strong." I rubbed my eyes and cringed as a fake eyelash came loose. "Shoot."

Gilly walked over, and with the calm only a BFF can bring, she took the eyelash from me. "Close your eyes."

I did.

She put the lash back in place, then swiped under my eye with her thumb to clear off any smudged liner or mascara. "There," she said. "All better. Now, explain your reasoning."

"There was too much…intensity for that memory to be play-acting."

"Maybe they were method actors," Gilly said. "You know, really living the part."

"You've seen these people act," Ezra noted. "Do you think any of them could pull off a real performance?"

Gilly winced. "No. I mean, they aren't terrible for what they've been hired for. But no, I don't think any of them could pull off what you're talking about, Nora."

"Even if they could, it doesn't explain the other visions, like the one with the kid and mom, or the crew of bullies. And there was the secretive hook-up in the library. This doesn't feel put on or fake. It feels super real." I pivoted my gaze to the door. "We should find Pippa and Jordy. We're going to have to gather as much information about all the players if we want to stop this couple's plan."

"Wait a minute," Scott said. "We can't exactly ask strangers if they're planning on murdering someone, and the actors are all playing roles. When we were interviewing them, they really stuck to their characters. How are we supposed to get them to reveal personal information?"

"Their real names are listed in the brochure. We can search the internet..." Gilly's shoulders dropped, and her lower lip jutted out. "Except, they have our freaking phones locked up somewhere."

"It's another good thought," Ezra said. "Having their real names is a start."

I snapped my fingers. "Maybe it's a married couple. And the woman and her lover are plotting to kill the husband."

"It's a cliché," said Ezra, "but it's also true. Most spousal murders are committed by partners."

"Okay. So, maybe we'll get lucky. If two of the actors have the same last name, that might give us our married couple and lead us to the probable victim."

Scott took the brochure from the dressing table. I think we were all holding our breaths as he read through it. At least, I was.

Finally, he looked up and gave a small head-shake. "No same last names."

"It can't ever be easy, can it?" I asked. "Let's lay out the potential victims." I grabbed the dry erase marker from the packet along with the blank page for notes. I made two columns. One for the men. Potential suspect-slash-victims. And one column for the women. Potential conspirators. "Okay, so we have Robert Forester, who plays the detective and the principal, Sawyer Johnson is Biff Cruise, Tim Dean who plays Brian Bender, and Tony Morton is Mr. Moore." I moved to the second set of names. "Wendy Price is Mary Jane Masterson, our brunette cheerleader, Lynn Gleason is Leah Standish, the blonde, Tina Rothschild is Mrs. Nelson."

"There could be more than one married couple in that group," Gilly said.

"Or no married couples," Scott added.

"Maybe the wife didn't take her husband's last name." Gilly shrugged. "Lots of women don't. And we haven't even considered if one or both of the suspects are from the guests and not the actors."

Ezra frowned. "We won't completely discount it."

"The scent of pot was fairly fresh," I said. "This wasn't a distant memory."

Gilly began to pace. "Unless the person who

smoked the pot recently had a memory about something that happened in the past when he or she smoked the pot before."

"Convoluted, but possible. Still, I'm not convinced." I tapped the marker on the paper. "The couple was making a plan to murder someone on opening weekend. This is opening weekend. The fact that it hasn't happened yet gives us the opportunity to stop it. An opportunity we don't usually get." This was the first time one of my scent visions had given me a warning of a crime, and I couldn't risk ignoring the metaphysical heads-up if it meant saving a life.

Gilly sat on the edge of the bed. "This wasn't the kind of mystery I had in mind for my birthday weekend."

"I wish my psychic smeller could be used as evidence so we could get the police involved." I glanced at Ezra. "And maybe if we were in Garden Cove, we might've had wiggle room." After all, I'd worked with the police on several investigations as a psychic consultant. "But this is a different town. Hell, it's a different county."

"But Easy's a detective," Gilly said. "Doesn't that give him some credibility, even if it's not his jurisdiction?"

Ezra shrugged and raised his hands palm up. "I

have one line from one of Nora's visions talking about killing someone. We don't have a victim or a suspect. It's not enough to call in the cavalry."

"You're right." Gilly sighed. "This isn't how I saw this weekend going." She looked up at Scott. "I'm sorry. I thought this would be a fun getaway for all of us."

The hot doc put his hand on her shoulder. "I've been having a great time. This is the first time I haven't been on call at the hospital in a year, and I get to be with you." He gave her a sympathetic smile. "What do you want to do?"

Gilly nodded. "Nora's right. If someone's in trouble, we have to help."

Ezra cleared his throat. "We need to set some ground rules for safety reasons. I don't want anyone putting themselves in danger. It's more of an ears-and-eyes-open situation. If you ask personal questions of the actors, keep them vague. Anything you learn, even if it doesn't seem relevant, bring it to me immediately. All information is good information, and just because something doesn't seem important by itself, it might be a smaller piece of a larger puzzle."

I looked at the digital clock near the bed. "It's almost nine. We have two hours until tonight's festivities end. If we don't find out anything before eleven, let's meet back here." I frowned. "And when we find Pippa and Jordy, we're going to have to fill them in."

Gilly got up. "I think Pip and Jordy bailed on the game."

"What do you mean? They left?"

Gilly smirked. "I'm pretty sure they're boinking."

I quirked a brow.

"You know, knocking boots. Doing the nasty." She broke out into a flawless cabbage patch. "Puh-push it real good. The Humpty dance." She wiggled her rear. "Doing the butt."

Ezra and Scott chuckled.

I couldn't keep the grin off my face. "I get it. They're having sex."

"Oww. Sexy, sexy," Gilly sang, adding a snake move to the end of her dance. She stopped and shrugged. "That's my guess, anyhow."

If Pip and Jordy were in their room bumping uglies, I totally envied them right now. I wasn't going to interrupt them for something that could turn into a wild goose chase. And besides, sometimes less was more when it came to a covert investigation. "Okay. We stay in pairs, though. No one goes off on their own."

Gilly snorted then raised her hands in surrender

when I narrowed my gaze at her. "That's sound advice."

"Just act like you're still doing the fake investigation," I said, choosing to ignore her sarcasm. Had I gotten caught on my own once or twice by a bad guy? Yes. Was it because I was stupid? Nope. More like wrong place, wrong time.

Gilly's face lit up with an idea. "Make sure you flatter them. They're small-town actors. They aren't doing this job for the money. They must love the work, even if they aren't great at it. I bet if we push the right buttons, someone will break character."

"Good idea," I concurred. "No situation was ever made worse by a little flattery. Just keep it friendly, so the baddies don't catch on to us."

Ezra clapped his hands and started toward the door. "Clock is ticking. We don't know how long we have before these two make their move."

"If they make it at all," Scott said. "Devil's advocate. They could've changed their minds about doing the deed. We could be worried for nothing."

"Here's hoping," I told him. "I'd really love for this to be a false alarm."

Gilly bumped me with her hip. "Whatever happens, we're in this together." She rubbed her palms and said, "Let's go find us a potential killer."

CHAPTER
EIGHT

Before we parted ways, the four of us decided to divide and conquer with the potential suspects and victims. Gilly and Scott would focus on Hughes, Nelson, and Moore. Ezra and I would take Leah, Brian, and Mary Jane. We all agreed that if any of us ran into Biff, we'd try to connect with the actor, but it didn't seem likely. I had a feeling the pretend corpse was the man behind the camera.

The gymnasium was still rocking with '80s music spilling out into the halls.

"If you were going to off your spouse or partner or whatever and make it look like an accident, how would you go about it?" I asked Ezra.

He gave me a sly grin. "I've never really thought about it."

"You weren't married long enough," I said with a

laugh.

"True." He chuckled. "This is a school, and there are lots of strings being pulled to make this mystery happen. But I'm just not sure what someone could do to make a real death look accidental. It's not as easy as people might think. And it's hard to kill someone without leaving any evidence behind."

"Tell that to the thousands of killers who get away with it every year."

"For now," he said, "but not forever. Look at all the cold cases being solved these days because of DNA."

"True." I pointed up the hall toward the offices. "Look, there's the detective guy. Only, he has on the gray wig, so I guess he's Principal Hughes now."

"Let's take the hall before the gym," Ezra said. "Scott and Gilly have him."

"You really don't like him, do you?"

"He raises my hackles. Still don't know why." We turned right before the corridor and headed down the hall toward the escape classrooms.

Once we were out of earshot of the other guests, I said, "Maybe he has done some television or movie acting. He reminds me of Jerry Orbach."

"The guy from *Law and Order*?"

"Yeah, him." I gave the tip of my nose a squeeze. "He's got the same honker."

Ezra choked on a laugh. "It's possible. But until I can settle it in my head, I don't want to spook him. You already said he's probably not the guy from the visions."

"Emphasis on probably."

"I trust your instincts."

I leaned my head on his shoulder as we walked up the corridor. "I love that about you."

"And here I thought you only loved me for my—"

"There you are!" a woman exclaimed, cutting Ezra off just as he was getting to the good stuff. I groaned as Velma and Daffney fast-walked in our direction. Velma waved her hand. "We've been looking everywhere for you, Nora."

I narrowed my gaze at her. "Why?"

My question seemed to take Velma aback. "Because, well, you know. To compare notes and catch up."

I felt bad for my abruptness. "Sorry, I didn't mean for that to come off the way it did. We're just really focused on the, uhm, game."

Daffney was gawking at Ezra. What was her deal with him? I mean, I got it. Ezra was a good-looking man. Even so, her interest seemed a little blatant considering I was standing right next to him. Daffney blushed when she noticed I'd caught her staring. She glanced away at the floor and said, "I'm sure you were busy. I told Velma not to bother, but you know how she is."

I didn't. I hadn't seen the sisters in over thirty years. I had no idea what either of them was like. "No worries. We can catch up tomorrow. Why don't you guys meet us for breakfast?"

Velma brightened. "Absolutely." She patted the air in front of me. "I can't wait to hear what you've been up to since the good old days."

Inwardly, I groaned. I wasn't one of those people who thought of the past as magical. I was grateful for all my experiences, but frankly, my best life was right now. "Great," I said.

"Ladies," he said as he took my hand. Ezra gave them a slight nod. "Later."

"Bye." I waved and let Ezra lead me away from the sisters. "Is Daffney acting suspicious, or is it just me?"

"She gives me the willies," Ezra said. "She keeps staring at me."

"Because you're a handsome guy." I tugged his beard. "Even with all this fur."

"Ow," he said, brushing the hair down. "As soon as the district attorney in Kansas City brings charges against the dockside drug ring, I'll shave."

We'd carpooled with Gilly, Pippa, Jordy, and

Scott, so we hadn't really had a chance to talk about what he'd gone through during his weeks in Kansas City or what it meant for him now that he was home. I had assumed he was done with all that business, but maybe not.

I frowned at him. "Is there a chance you'll have to go back? I mean, undercover."

"Not too likely."

"But there is a chance."

"A slight one." He put his arm around my shoulders and gave my upper arm an affectionate tickle. "I don't want you to worry, though."

"Easier said than done." I patted his hand. "How about I stop worrying when you get to shave?"

"Deal," he said. He leaned over and brushed his beard against my cheek.

I giggled. "Stop."

The hallway door to the back of the gym was open. I saw the Flock of Seagulls guy and the blonde cheerleader walk through the kitchen doors. He looked like a man on a mission.

"Hey, there's two of our suspects." I gestured toward the gym. "Real names are Tim Dean and Lynn Gleason, I think."

"Good memory," Ezra said. "Let's go see if they're the lovers we're looking for.

We hurried down the hall to the open door.

There was so much noise from the gym, I wasn't too worried about being overheard. We quickly moved through the doors into the kitchen.

I heard muffled voices in the back but couldn't make out what they were saying.

Ezra gestured to get my attention then mouthed the word, "Closer."

I nodded, grateful I was wearing sneakers and not clunky, clackity heels as we advanced forward. I turned sideways to shimmy around a wire rack of pots and pans and snagged my dress on a utensil hook. The action jostled a crate of drinking glasses. I let out a barely audible hiss as I eased back and detached myself from the metal prong. Ezra raised his brows in a question.

I gave him the OK sign. The voices were coming from behind a closed door. I held up a finger for Ezra to wait. I went back to the crate with glasses and took two of them from their slots. I carried them back to Ezra and handed him one.

He smirked and whispered. "Kickin' it old school."

I grinned. "Every chance I get."

He gave me a quick kiss before putting the open side of the glass to the door. I did the same with mine. The muffled conversation became clearer.

"It's going good, right?" I heard Lynn ask. "Other

than the two who broke the locked drawer in the chemistry room, everyone seems to be having a good time."

"One guy already made a guess," Tim Dean said. "He was wrong, of course."

"I overheard Nellie Lox say she wanted to put our weekend on her Pinstabook channel. Maybe we should've let them keep their phones."

"We all agreed, Lynn. Cellphones give an unfair advantage to players."

"I know," she whined. "But we've sunk everything into this place..."

"We're booked through to the end of the summer," he assured her. "I promise, babe. We're going to make this work. The only real option, for all of us, is success." There was a short pause. "Haven't I always taken care of you?"

"You're right," she said.

"What was going on with Buzz and T earlier?" Tim asked.

"Creative differences," Lynn said quickly. "Don't worry about them. I'll handle it."

A clang of pans followed by a sharp curse startled me. I dropped the glass on the floor, and it bounced against the door.

"What was that?" The words were loud, sharp, and unmistakable on the other side of the door.

Ezra set his glass on a shelf and pulled me into his arms and away from the door. He turned me until my back was against the wall, and before I could yelp, he sealed my mouth with a passionate kiss.

The door opened. "Who's out here?"

"Damn it to hell," a man groused. "My trousers have been eviscerated."

"Is that you, Bob?" Tim demanded.

"Of course, it's me, you moronic twit." The overhead lights flickered on as someone flipped a switch. "Why are there two people making out next to canned goods?"

Oops. Caught.

My lids flickered open and staring back at me were the most gorgeous green eyes. In the two years we'd been together, I never tired of this view. Ezra eased back from the kiss. "Hello, gorgeous," he said.

"Hello, sexy," I replied.

"What are you two doing back here?" Lynn demanded. She had on a pair of sparkling earrings in the shape of bees and a necklace pendant to match. Very cute and young jewelry, fitting for her cheerleader character. She nervously tugged at her necklace. "This area is off-limits to guests."

Ezra straightened his jacket. "Excuse us. We were…uh…looking for some place private."

"Your rooms are private," Lynn said.

"Sorry." I held up my hands. "We haven't seen each other for a few weeks..."

Tim's expression softened. "It's not a problem, really. The kitchen and the staff hallway are restricted for a reason, though."

"Sorry," Ezra said. "We'll get out of your hair now."

"I didn't mean to sound harsh. Flashbacks," Lynn added on a laugh. "But I'm not a teacher anymore, and you all aren't two lovesick teens caught making out in the kitchen."

The actor who'd played Biff, Sawyer Johnson, came in behind Robert Forester—or Bob, as Lynn had called him. He smirked when he saw us. "You two." He shook his head. "Get a room."

Bob moved forward and knocked stuff over on a shelf. The man wasn't steady on his feet. "I can't work under these conditions, Dean." He shook a fist at Lynn and Tim. " My life was nearly snuffed out."

"By what?" I asked automatically.

"When I was doing a quick change, I slipped on the floor. I could have been concussed! Some imbecile spilled oil on the..." His words trailed off as he glanced around the room at all of us, then shook his head. "Never mind."

"Excuse us," Tim said to Ezra and me. He

gestured toward the exit. "It ruins the illusion if you peek behind the curtain. I hope you understand."

I nodded. "Yeah, definitely."

The actress playing Ms. Nelson, Tina Rothschild, was at the kitchen entrance. She looked mildly surprised to see Ezra and me walking toward her.

"The kitchen is staff only," she said.

I nodded. "We were just leaving."

After we passed by her, I heard her say, "Watch what you're doing."

I turned back sharply to see Bob throwing his shoulders back and straightening his suit. "Pardon me," he muttered.

"Arrogant lush," Tina sneered. "If I'd wanted to babysit dickheads, I would have kept teaching teenagers." Her gaze pivoted to me, and she forced a smile that didn't reach her eyes.

Ezra looped his arm with mine. "I think that's our cue to go."

"Yep," I agreed.

After we made our way out of the cafeteria, Ezra asked, "Do you think Ms. Nelson..." He let the question hang.

I picked it up. "...is our mysterious Mrs. P from the vision?"

Ezra nodded.

"She's definitely at the top of the list."

CHAPTER
NINE

While the trip to the kitchen hadn't produced any revealing information or additional visions, we'd learned a few things. One, both Lynn Gleason and Tina Rothschild had been teachers, Lynn and Tim Dean had sunk all their money into this place and were in financial straits, and Robert Forester was supremely pompous. And quite possibly a drunkard. I'd estimated his age at late fifties, early sixties. Older than everyone else in the cast.

His speech pattern in the kitchen had reminded me of actors like David Odgen Stiers from *M.A.S.H*, or John Larroquette, from *Night Court*. I'd read once that Larroquette had developed his voice for radio. In other words, it had been an affectation, not his natural speaking voice. Forester had smoothly switched his voice between Principal Hughes and Tubbs Crockett, both different from the voice he'd projected in the kitchen.

"Come on," I said. "Let's go stalk Mr. Moore." Aka Tony Morton.

"Who do you think Buzz is?" Ezra asked.

"Buzz?"

"The woman said that Buzz and T had creative differences."

"That's right," I told him. "Tim Dean asked what was up between those two actors."

Ezra took the playbill from his jacket pocket. "My memory is not nearly as sharp as yours." He smiled. "There are three Ts, Tina, Tim, and Tony. We can rule out Tim because he's the one who asked the question."

"And Buzz." I pointed to a name on the actor list. I rattled out my thought process. "Sawyer Johnson. Sawyer. Saw. Buzzsaw. Buzz."

"Probably. There's also Wendy Price. You said in the memory that the guy called the woman Mrs. P. Could it have been Wendy, instead?"

"Possibly," I admitted. "It sounded like Winnie, but the names are similar." I let out a growl of frustration. "This is the opening weekend. If the memory is right, that couple is plotting someone's death." I threw my hands up. "What's the use of having this stupid psychic nose? Right now, it feels like a curse."

"Nora," Ezra said softly. "It's a gift." He cupped my face with his palm. "You've helped the police put away some really bad people, and in the process, you've saved lives."

"But this is the first time we might be able to stop a murder. I don't want to be part of the clean-up crew after the crime has been committed. If I can't do that..."

"Honestly, Nora, we might not be able to stop whatever is going to happen. But, babe, it won't be your fault. People are unpredictable. You can't control what they do."

"I know you're right." *You can't control the way other people behave*, I'd told my goddaughter when her father had been arrested. *You can only control the way you react to their behavior*. Those words of wisdom I'd imparted to the teenager were not bringing me comfort now. "It doesn't make me feel better." Still, I managed to force a smile. "We'll get the bad guys."

Ezra nodded. "Okay. Where to next?"

Over the intercom, someone said, "All students, please go to the gymnasium."

"Well, damn. Our *density* has been decided for us."

He chuckled at my *Back to the Future* joke. "Come on, McFly."

The gymnasium was still an artsy craftsy winter wonderland. The music was still playing, the lights had been dimmed again, and the disco ball was bouncing light everywhere. Suddenly, three spotlights hit the center court, lighting up Detective Crockett, A Flock of Seagulls dude, and both cheerleaders. Mr. Moore and Ms. Nelson stood nearby.

The music's volume lowered, rendering it background noise.

"Part two of clues," Gilly said as she sidled in next to me. "Did you find out anything new?"

"Maybe. How about you?"

"Nothing that screamed murder," she said quietly. "Talk after?"

"Definitely."

"I have a few questions," Forester declared. The phony detective addressed A Flock of Seagulls first. "Mr. Bender, where were you when Biff Cruise was killed?" His voice was amplified over the speakers.

"Ms. Nelson took me out the back of the gym," Bender answered. He was easily heard as well, which meant the actors were probably miked. "I wasn't anywhere near the office. Or the library."

"I left Mr. Bender to cool off," Ms. Nelson said. "I

can't account for his whereabouts during the time leading up to Biff's...death." She sniffled. "Poor Biff."

Bender turned a glare in her direction. "Why would I kill him?" He grabbed the brunette cheerleader, Mary Jane, around the waist and tugged her to him. "I already got the girl."

She slapped him, and whoever was running the sound effects was doing a brilliant job because we all heard the crack bounce around the gym. "He's dead because of you," she said before turning on the blonde cheerleader. "And you! How could you tell him about Brian and me?"

The blonde sneered. "I didn't have to tell him," she said. "He already knew." She pointed at Bender. "Biff said he would kill him. But Brian strangled him first!"

"Ms. Standish." Crockett walked over to her. He pushed up the sleeves on his pastel jacket. "From what I've heard, you had a fight with Biff yesterday during study hall. Witnesses say you fled the classroom in tears. You wanna tell me what that was about?"

"It was...it was nothing," she stammered.

Ms. Nelson put her arm around the blonde. "Don't badger her, Detective. Can't you see she's upset?"

"That's enough." Mr. Moore stepped forward. "I

can't believe any of our students would kill Biff. He was a shining example in this school."

The detective turned his gaze dramatically to the blonde cheerleader. "Is that true, Ms. Standish? Was Biff a shining example?"

"Biff knew a lot of things," Leah said. "He...he knew stuff about people. Stuff he used to get his way." She crossed her arms over her chest. "I don't know who killed him or why." Fat tears rolled down her cheeks. "But I'm not sorry he's dead. And anyone here says different, then you know they're lying."

Two of the spotlights went out, and all the actors but Tubbs Crockett took a step back, leaving the fake detective in the single circle of light. "Biff Cruise was a keeper of dirty secrets. If you want to find who killed him, you must uncover the information the murderer wants buried."

The lighting dimmed again. But it was enough light to see that the other five actors were gone. The volume of the music cranked back up to a dull roar.

"I didn't see them go," I said. "I was too busy watching the detective."

"That's the magic of showbiz." Gilly sighed. "I'm really bummed. This murder plot would be a lot more fun if we weren't looking for an actual almost murderer. I really wanted bragging rights."

"If we stop someone from really dying this

weekend," Ezra told her. "I'll let you read the Miranda rights."

Her brows raised, and her eyes widened. "Really?"

"Can a citizen read a criminal the Miranda rights?" Scott asked. "That doesn't seem like it would hold up in court."

Gilly's lower lip jutted. "Spoilsport."

"I'm curious, is all," Scott said. "If you want, I'll let you read me my Miranda rights later tonight."

"You have the right to remain sexy," Gilly told him.

I choked on a laugh. "They must've amended the Miranda Act since the last time I heard it."

"Yep." Ezra gave me a quick wink. He looked at Scott. "I'm outside of my jurisdiction, so any arrest we make will have to be a citizen's arrest until the Button Falls PD can send someone out here to take whoever into custody."

"This means we have to catch them in the act, doesn't it?" Scott asked.

I shook my head. "We just need proof of a plot."

Ezra nodded. "It's called conspiracy to commit murder, and it'll get the perps life in prison, same as if they committed first-degree murder."

"We're going to definitely need more than my nose to prove it to the local police."

Gilly nodded. "So, what did you guys find out?"

"That at least two of the actors used to be teachers. Lynn Gleason and Tina Rothschild."

"The one playing Ms. Nelson gives me Loverlegs flashbacks," Gilly said. "You remember that old battle-ax, Nora?"

Indeed, I did. "Mrs. Lovergorn." I grimaced. "She gave me a C minus in civics because I mixed up a couple of words when we had to recite the constitution's preamble."

"She was definitely prickly." Gilly snickered. "Which is why we called her Loverlegs. She always had leg hair poking out of her stockings."

"She sounds delightful," Scott said.

"In her defense," Gilly added, "the older I get, the more I can see the appeal of not shaving or waxing."

"Don't make me get out the weed eater," I told Gilly. "Because I will if you stop shaving."

Scott laughed. "You'd be cute even if you were hairy."

"You've never slept in the same bed with a hairy Gilly," I countered. "That thick hair on her head translates to the rest of her."

"Nora!" Gilly exclaimed. Then she giggled. "It's true. The hairs on my legs are lethal weapons when they grow out."

"Not that all this hair talk isn't interesting," Ezra interrupted. "But we only have about an hour before lights out and we lose access to the suspects, fake and real. We should mingle and see what we can find out."

Before we split up, Pippa and Jordy walked into the left front doors of the gym. Jordy's long hair was pulled back into a thick ponytail, and Pippa's permed wig looked slightly cockeyed.

"Guess the lovebirds finally came up for air." I waved at our slightly disheveled friends. I knew they'd been struggling as new parents to make time for intimacy. Jordy waved back, but Pippa made a beeline for the Pinstabook celebrity. "We should tell them what's going on."

Gilly nudged me. "You're going to have to pry her away from that Nellie Lox woman, first."

Ezra gestured toward Pippa and the influencer. "Why don't you and Gilly grab Pip, and Scott and I will get Jordy up to speed. We'll meet out in the hallway."

"Sounds good to me," I said.

"Me too," Gilly agreed. She gave Scott a kiss on the cheek. "Don't miss me too much."

He laughed. "Impossible."

Gilly was all smiles as we walked away.

"So," I said, giving her shoulder a bump. "Things are getting pretty serious, eh?"

"He told me he loved me," she revealed.

I stopped and turned Gilly to face me. Her grin widened as I gave her a *squee* of delight. "I can't believe you are just now telling me!"

"It just happened like half an hour ago. Believe me, if I would've had my phone, you would've been my first text."

"What's going on?" Pippa asked. "You both look like you're sitting on a bomb."

"Scott told Gilly he loved her," I blurted out.

"Nora!" Gilly exclaimed. "That's my news."

I winced. "Sorry."

"Eeeeee!" Pippa's squeal of delight matched my own. "How, when, where?"

Gilly shushed us and looked around to make sure the guys weren't in earshot. "The normal way, about half an hour ago, and in the History Room. We were following the detective actor and ducked in there to keep from being seen when he turned around and headed back to the gym." She narrowed her gaze on Pippa's crooked lace-front wig, then reached out and straightened it. "He'd pulled me into the room, and like some romantic comedy, I fell into his arms. We both laughed. Then he said 'I love you, Gillian Martin.'"

"Awww," Pippa and I said simultaneously.

"And then you said?" I asked.

"I gave him two thumbs up and offered to review him on Yelp." She laughed and shook her head. "I told him I loved him back, of course."

I grabbed her hand and gave her a serious look. "And you do, right? You do love him?"

"I really do, Nora. I love him in a take-him-home-to-meet-the-kids kind of way."

I embraced her. Pippa threw her slender arms around the both of us.

"Group hug," a woman said before adding her arms to the mix. "What are we celebrating?"

Pippa disengaged, and we all glanced at our clingy intruder. It was Nellie Lox.

"Pippa, introduce me to your friends," she said. "I am so bored, and I need someone to spill the tea this instant."

"Oh." Pippa blushed. "This is Nora and Gilly." She gestured to us. "Nora and Gilly, meet Nellie."

"Hi, Nellie," I said. "Nice to meet you."

"Yeah." Gilly's tone was suspicious. "Nice to meet you."

"Enough of the small talk, ladies." The social influencer let us go. "Dish already. Did someone get engaged?"

"Not engaged," Pippa started.

Gilly pinched her upper arm.

"Ow." She rubbed the spot. "Got it. Not my news to tell."

I was giggling when I smelled the strong cologne from earlier. "Oh." I reached out and grabbed Gilly's sleeve. "Oh, no."

"It smells so awful in here," a woman says. She reaches into her purse and spritzes the air around her and the man next to her. The lighting is dim wherever they are, and while I can't see their faces because I never do, I also can't make out any clear details about their clothes. "There. That's a little better. Why are we here?"

The guy tells her, "I got a foolproof plan, P. All you have to do is get him here."

"And then what?"

"Carbon monoxide poisoning. Over four hundred people die in the United States every year from it."

"That's a really specific number. How do you know this?"

"I looked it up on the internet."

"You're so smart," she says with an overly complimentary tone. "Though, make sure you scrub your search history."

He pulls her close. "Already done."

She reaches up and, from what I can tell, taps him on the nose. "I'm so lucky."

He dips his head to hers. "Oh, bear. How I do love you."

"And I love you, my Christopher."

"Carbon monoxide. Oh, bear. How I do love you," I muttered as the vision went away and the gym reappeared. I was on the ground with my head in Gilly's lap. Pippa was fanning me, and Nellie had my feet in her arms, raising them up in the air. The guys had shown up sometime during the intense memory and were keeping everyone away from me, even the actors who were gawking at me along with the guests.

"Should we call an ambulance?" Tina Rothschild, aka Ms. Nelson, asked. "We have a land line in the office."

"I'm okay." Nellie let go of my legs, and Gilly helped me sit up. Ezra hauled me to my feet. "I get these spells sometimes. Nothing to worry about."

"Do you have a seizure disorder?" Tim asked. "It's in the brochure that we use strobe lights."

"Not seizures, exactly," I assured him. "I'm okay. Please, everyone, go back to your fun." I needed to get my friends away from this very public space and tell them what I found out. I still didn't know the victim, but at least now I knew the means for death. Carbon monoxide poisoning. "I need a little air. You all could come with me." I gave them a meaningful look.

"Absolutely." Gilly rubbed my back. "Let's get some air."

"Hey," Nellie said. "Why were you quoting *Winnie-the-Pooh*?"

"I was doing what?" I asked.

"*Winnie-the-Pooh*," she said again. "You know, the *Oh, bear. How I do love you.*" I must've been staring at her like she'd grown a third nostril because she added, "You don't raise three children and not memorize certain books. And that one is a favorite of my eldest."

Cripes. Was that the key? Was the P in Mrs. P for Pooh? The guy had called her Winnie. And she'd called him Chris. Christopher. For Christopher Robin. Code names? Pet names? And if Winnie-the-Pooh and Christopher Robin were planning on killing someone… I felt sick to my stomach.

"I…I *really* need fresh air." I clung to Ezra. "Get me out of here. Now."

CHAPTER
TEN

The cool, brisk air filled my lungs. It had started to snow, and I welcomed the chill against my hot face.

"What did you see?" Ezra asked after I'd had a moment to gather my wits.

Gilly, Scott, Pippa, and Jordy were in a half-circle in front of us, acting as a screen against any Nosy Rosies who might be looking at us from the school.

"We can go," Gilly said. "You don't owe anyone anything."

"But if someone gets killed, I'd never forgive myself," I told her. "And neither would you."

"Argh! You're right. But these memories are knocking you for a loop."

"The fresher and more emotional they are, the

more intense they get," I said. I took in more deep breaths. "I feel better now that we're outside."

"What in the ever-loving hell is going on?" Pippa asked. "Am I missing something?"

"Nora's seeing memories of someone plotting murder," Gilly informed her.

Pippa stared at me, her lips pursed tightly. "Of course, you are," she finally said. She looked at Jordy. "We should've stayed in the room."

Jordy ran his hand over the top of his head. "That's still an option." He didn't sound like he was joking. I couldn't blame him. Our last investigation had put Pippa in grave danger. Of course, Jordy would be freaked out by that.

I put my hand on Pippa's arm. "You don't have to be involved. I'm happy to have you out of harm's way."

Her gaze narrowed on me and the lines between her brows deepened. "If you're involved, then I am, too." She pivoted her eyes to Jordy. "And don't you dare try to stop me."

He raised a hand in surrender. "I never would." Still, he didn't look happy about it.

Pippa studied him for a moment, then, as if satisfied with his answer, she nodded and turned to me. "Tell me what's going on, and don't leave anything out."

Between Gilly and me, we managed to get Pippa up to speed in a couple of minutes. I told her about all the visions and what little we had learned when we'd gotten caught in the kitchen.

"Oh," Gilly added, "I found out that Mr. Moore is gay. I think that means we can exclude him from the suspect and victim pool, right?"

"How'd you find that out?" I asked.

"Courtesy of Daffney Graves. She was flirting hard with him to the point that it made me uncomfortable. Finally, he ended up telling her that his boyfriend thought he had a cute butt, too." She giggled. "I nearly peed myself."

"There is something shifty about Daffney," Ezra said.

"Is she a suspect?" Pippa asked. "I mean, could she be?"

"I don't think so." I shook my head. "She wants to talk to me in private, but I doubt it's because she's planning to tell me about a murder plot. Besides, I'm pretty sure she's single. The woman we're looking for has at least two lovers."

"One she's banging and one she wants to murder," Gilly stated.

I nodded in the affirmative. "We have three women in the cast, the two cheerleaders and the teacher. And there are four men, the principal, the teacher, the student, and stiff." I didn't bring up the other guests as possible suspects, but the psychic memories led me to believe the couple who were plotting had much closer ties to the event. "Oh, and the teacher claims to have a boyfriend. If it's true, it will rule him out."

"Hmm," Pippa said. "I had a friend in college who would tell aggressively forward guys that she was a lesbian, so they would leave her alone. He could've been lying."

"Maybe." I didn't think so, though. People in rural areas weren't always the most progressive or the most accepting when it came to sexuality. "I'm not convinced he'd lie about it if it wasn't true, but we won't cross Morton off the list."

"You mean Moore," Pippa said.

"His real name is Tony Morton." Ezra retrieved the playbill from his pocket. "Here's the cheat sheet."

Jordy frowned. "It might be easier to use their character names for now. At least, until we find more information."

Scott cast Jordy a grateful glance. "The multiple names are confusing."

"All right," Ezra said. "Far be it from me to make things more complicated."

A smirk tugged at my lips. "Bringing the complicated is my job."

"Babe," Ezra's eyes softened, "you're just the right amount of complicated."

The night air had sunk a chill into my skin, but Ezra's gaze warmed me. He glanced up at the school entrance. "We have one lead. The means. The would-be killer is planning to use carbon monoxide as his weapon of choice. There can't be that many places in a school where a CO death would be ruled an accident."

"I agree," I said. "But I'm not sure the guy is all that bright. These visions have had a very *Romeo and Juliet* tragedy feel about them. Between the old-fashioned cologne and the creepy Winnie-the-Pooh references, there's a real sense of emotional immaturity with both the man and the woman."

"Do you think she's really in danger?" Gilly tugged at her lower lip. "I mean, from her other lover, husband, or whatever? She said she was scared of him, right? Or am I misremembering that?" One of Gilly's exes had been abusive and stalkery before he'd ended up dead. Neither one of us had been sorry to see that son-of-a-creep gone for good. Still, Gilly wouldn't have killed him herself. Not unless she'd had to in self-defense.

I, however, had pulled a gun on the guy. The ex-jerk had filed a restraining order against me, which is how I met Ezra Holden. He'd been the cop to serve me the papers.

"I don't know." My teeth chattered as the winter weather seeped into my bones. "She acted as if that was the case, but the woman didn't come right out and say it."

"You're shaking," Ezra said. He opened his jacket for me, and I slid my arms inside.

"It's getting cold out here," I said.

"We should get back inside," Gilly said. "What's the plan?"

"Pippa and Jordy stay in the common areas and keep an eye out for suspicious movements from the actors or guests," Ezra said. "If you see something, don't follow them. Come and get me, instead."

I caught the grateful look Jordy passed to Ezra, but I was glad Pippa hadn't seen it. She hated being treated like a fragile butterfly. Still, watching the cast of suspects and potential victims was an important role.

"Agreed," I said. "None of us should chase down any wannabe killers on our own. Safety in numbers and all that."

"Gilly, Scott, Nora, and I will do a quick sweep of the halls," Ezra said.

The older actor, Forester, had said something

about spilled oil when he was doing a quick change. Which meant it had probably happened in the areas that were off-limits to guests. "Can oil cause carbon monoxide poisoning?"

"If used as fuel," Jordy answered. "Most fuel sources can put off carbon monoxide. I had an old natural gas water heater that set off my CO monitors once."

"That was before I moved in." Pippa bounced on her toes and rubbed her arms to ward off the cold. "It was too small, so we got rid of it."

Jordy smiled at Pippa. "Because you kept using up all the hot water."

She grinned. "Like I said. Too small."

He put his arm around her shoulders. "Speaking of heat," he said. "We should move this inside."

We, as a group, started for the door.

"Other ways to get carbon monoxide poisoning are from cars, portable heaters, charcoal grills, and stoves," Scott added as we walked toward the school. "I don't know if that helps any, but from my experience in the emergency department at the hospital, those are the most common reasons I've seen."

Ezra nodded. "That is helpful."

Coming into the heated school was a relief. Pippa and Jordy headed toward the gym to catalog the whereabouts of our potential killers. But before the rest of us could covertly do our own snooping, we were instantly accosted by Tony Morton.

"Are you okay?" Morton asked. "We can call an ambulance if you need it."

"I'm okay," I told him.

Scott stepped in. "I'm a doctor," he told the actor. "I think Nora just got dehydrated."

"That's it," I agreed. "Getting outside for a minute helped."

"Maybe you should go back to your room," Morton said. "Just until you're sure you won't have another...incident." More quietly, he added, "I'm not sure we can afford to take a hit with the insurance company. We're already paying high premiums. I know that's not your problem, but...I'll be happy to send ice water to your room. I could probably scrounge up a sports drink as well to get those electrolytes replenished."

"You sound like the science teacher," I told him.

He chuckled. "I taught physical education."

"Really?" Pippa asked.

Morton shook his head and grinned. "Nah, I taught drama and ran the theater club for Button Falls High School."

"And now?"

"And now I do this," he said. He smiled, no

longer caring whether he stayed in character or not. "It's a risky venture, but so far, so good." He shrugged and did a head tilt. "The fainting aside"

"Honestly," Gilly said. "You guys have done a great job." She gave his arm a flirty, gentle poke. "So, you are one of the owners? I love the name. *School's Out for Murder*. That's fabulous." She cast a semi-apologetic look back at her doctor beau. His eyes were alight with amusement.

Morton seemed amused as well. "Thanks," he said. "My partner came up with the name?"

"Your boyfriend?" I asked, remembering that Gilly had overheard him say something along those lines to Daffney.

He arched a brow at me. "Because I'm a theater teacher?"

"Uh, no. Not at all," I stammered.

Morton chuckled again. "Kidding. I'm totally gay."

"Totally," Gilly said.

"I'm currently single." He inclined his head to Gilly. "If your doctor has a hot brother."

The highest giggle I'd ever heard tittered out of Gilly. I couldn't contain my snorting laugh.

"No brother," Scott said. "But I do have a sister who likes flannel a whole lot."

This comment made us all laugh.

The lines around Morton's eyes softened as he looked at me again. "I'm glad to see you're all right. If you feel lightheaded again..."

I gave him a two-finger salute. "I'll alert my medical staff."

He returned the gesture. "You do that."

Lynn Gleason, in her cheerleading uniform, came up behind Morton. She draped her arm over his shoulder. "Mr. Moore, Principal Hughes wants to see you." She gave him a coy smile. "He sounds ticked off."

"Let him know I'm on my way," Morton said, back in character. "He doesn't...know, does he?" He winked in our direction. "You know. About us?"

Lynn looked shocked, and I couldn't tell if it was real or acting. "Well, gotta jet. Talk later." And the cheerleader bounded off back into the gym.

Morton's gaze sharpened on me. "That's the only hint you're going to get from me. Do with it what you will." On that note, he followed the bubbly brunette.

"Oh. Em. Gee!" Gilly said. "Biff was blackmailing Mr. Moore because he was sleeping with a student."

CHAPTER
ELEVEN

"I really want to get a look at the staff quarters," I told Ezra as we walked down the hall toward the escape rooms. "Do you think they are all ex-teachers?"

"Maybe," he replied. "I still can't shake the feeling that I've seen that Forester guy before. Every time I see him, I feel..." He wrung his hands for a moment. "I feel rage. Like he's done something to me personally, but for the life of me, I can't put my finger on it."

"Are you sure he's not on some fugitive wanted list somewhere?"

"I wish I knew for certain," Ezra answered. "But my reaction to him is more personal. I don't get it, and it's really doing my head in."

"You've had an extreme couple of weeks." I laced

my fingers through his. "Maybe this weekend was a bad idea."

With a swift move, Ezra turned into me, his free arm encircled my waist, and he yanked me against his body. He stole my breath with a kiss that warmed me from my cheeks to my toes. I surrendered to desire, sliding my hands around his back. When the kiss ended, he pressed his forehead to mine. "The only bed I want to stay in this weekend is yours. If you're here, I'm here. I've missed you so damn much."

"I've missed you too." I sighed. "I worry about you, is all."

"I'm right as rain, darling," he assured me. "And I'm right where I want to be."

"Okay." I nodded, then smiled up at him. "So, do we want to try and sneak into the staff area?" I raised up on my toes and gave him a quick kiss. "Have a little looksie at the other side of the school?"

"Without a hall pass?" he teased. He kissed the tip of my nose. "For you, I'll risk detention."

"My hero."

"How are we going to get over there without being seen?"

"We'll have to go through the gym," I said, "and use the back left-side door. The one across from this one." I pointed to the gym door closest to the kitchen at the end of the hall.

Ezra nodded. "We'll need a distraction, though, if we want to sneak through there without being noticed."

"I think I know a fifty-four-year-old distraction that might just fit the bill." Gilly was clever, quick, and naturally a klutz. On her first date with Scott, she managed to set herself on fire then get tackled into a reflection pool by the hot doc to put out the flames. I didn't need anything so dramatic tonight, so I was pretty sure she could handle it. "I think she and Scott can come up with something. We'll stand near the door and have Pippa and Jordy keep a lookout. We'll go after Gilly causes a commotion, and all the players are engaged and distracted."

Ezra grinned. "You should've been a spy."

"Just don't go humming the theme from *Mission Impossible*."

"No promises," Ezra said. "Come on. Let's put the plan in action."

"You're a good sport."

"Team Nora." He brushed his shoulder against mine. "You think Gilly will catch herself on fire again?"

I giggled. "I think she'll be able to come up with

something less hazardous." Although, as it turned out, I'd underestimated Gilly.

"Yassss," my BFF, sister from another mister, and platonic life partner said with a snap. "I say we go full-on *Dirty Dancing*."

"That's too dangerous," I told her. "You haven't tried anything like that since we were in high school."

"Uhm, I beg to differ," Gilly countered. "I timed-of-my-lifed it at my thirtieth birthday party."

"I hate to be the one to point this out, but that was twenty-four years ago. I want a distraction, but not one that lands you in the hospital."

Gilly responded by sticking her tongue out at me.

"We can do it," Scott said with more confidence than I was feeling. "Besides, it's not like I have to hold her up over my head, right? She leaps, and we both go down."

"Exactly," Gilly added. "Then screaming, yelling, cussing. Blah, blah, blah. Fake an ankle injury—"

"Hopefully fake," I muttered.

Gilly ignored me. "People come running.

Distraction, distraction. Pippa gives you the thumbs up, and you both go."

"Okay," I agreed reluctantly. "But don't hurt yourself for real."

"I only hurt myself for real on days that end in Y," Gilly said. She gave me a quick hug. "Don't worry about me. I'll be fine. Promise. I'm going to go put a request in with the DJ." She turned me away from her then gave my tush a light slap. "Now, go tell Pippa the plan and get ready."

Pippa and Jordy positioned themselves at the midway point of the gym against the wall. They looked like extras from Mötley Crüe's "Smokin In The Boys' Room" video. In other words, way too cool for school. I shook my head when Pippa gave me two sharp thumbs up to indicate she was ready, completely blowing her coolness factor. Jordy, on the other hand, could dress like Steve Urkel from *Family Matters* and would still look like the bad boy every girl wanted to bang in the '80s. Luckily for my friend, looks were deceiving. Jordy was a genuinely good guy.

"It's about time." Ezra glanced at his watch.

"Uh-huh." I picked at the skin around my

thumbnail, nervously waiting for Gilly and Scott to make their move.

"She'll be okay," Ezra said.

"We're talking about the same girl who broke a date's foot with a bowling ball," I countered.

"Fair enough," Ezra smirked. "But Scott knows what's coming. He'll be fine too."

"Relax" by Frankie Goes to Hollywood ended, and the DJ's voice came over the loudspeakers. "This song is a dedication from Gilly to Nora. Gilly says, no one puts baby in the corner." There were whoops of excitement from the guests as Bill Medley's velvet-toned voice slow-crooned the words, *Now, I've had...*

"This is it," I told Ezra.

"Come on," he said. He took my hand, and we started toward the back, near the cafeteria line exit and across from the "Staff Only" door to the west-wing hall.

Gilly and Scott began to do a dirty Mambo that looked as if they'd been dancing together for years.

"Nice," Ezra commented. "They look good."

"They sure do," I observed. Gilly had always been a great dancer. The woman had more rhythm in her pinkie toe than I had in my whole body, but I hadn't really seen her let go like this in a very long time. Even so, I was surprised by how well she grooved. Scott, on the other hand, was a masterful surprise. He had Patrick Swayze's moves down. "I'm impressed."

Ezra nodded. "Me too."

The guests on the dance floor parted, and the non-dancers had started to take notice as my bestie and her guy brought the big finale home. The crescendo of the song began to play, and a flutter of anxiety rose in my gut. "I'm not sure this is a good idea." The song hit the *this could be love* portion, and I held my breath. Ezra's grip firmed as the crowd of guests parted.

Gilly, without hesitation, ran toward Scott, arms held out like a crane ready to take flight, and leapt.

A collective gasp echoed throughout the gym as the couple went down.

I cast an anxious glance from the hot mess in the center of the gym to Pippa and Jordy. Pippa looked as worried as me, but Jordy, a cooler head, gave us the go-ahead.

Ezra grabbed the door handle, opened the door enough to squeeze through, and pulled me into the dark hallway after him.

We waited in silence for a few seconds to see if anyone had seen us. If we were going to get caught, we wanted it to be sooner rather than later. No one had followed us.

"Do you think she's okay?" I whispered.

Ezra nodded. "I'm sure Scott's taking good care of her."

"Probably." I know I sounded pouty, but I couldn't help myself. "I just worry, is all."

Ezra gave me a one-armed shoulder hug. "I know you do. But we need to focus on the mission." He gave me a teasing smile. "Don't let her sacrifice be for nothing."

I snorted a laugh. "All right." As we moved down the hallway, the lights flickered on. "Yikes. So much for hiding in the shadows."

"They must be connected to motion sensors." He glanced around. "Let's just get around the corner in case someone comes out of the gym."

The first door we saw on the back hall was marked, Custodian. "Jordy said anything that could be used as fuel. Do you think any of the cleaning supplies could cause carbon monoxide poisoning?"

Ezra rattled the handle. "Locked," he said. "But we'll keep it as a possibility."

The next door wasn't marked, but it was cracked open. "Here." I ducked inside. The room was situated with four makeup tables with vanity mirrors, wig forms, and other accessories. Each one had a small swivel chair in front. And there was a rack on the far side of the room with suits, jeans, letter jackets, and shirts hanging from a horizontal pole.

Ezra gestured at the items. "Sniff around. Maybe you'll get a hit."

I nodded. "Maybe." I knew it was the right thing to do, but the memories I'd been experiencing had taken a physical toll. The first table had a glass water bottle with an umbrella on the side and a flip-top straw lid, stage makeup, a jar of cold cream, and a half-eaten candy bar. The second table had similar items, with the addition of a coffee mug with the letters *HG* and the words, *a hug without you is toxic*. The last table had a feathered blond wig, it wreaked of cologne, and there was a makeup case near the center. "That must be Robert Forester's area."

I opened the case and grabbed a foundation compact, sniffed it, and wrinkled my nose. It smelled slightly like homemade Play-Doh, but it didn't stir up any emotional energy. Next, I picked up a tube of lip balm. It carried the scent of synthetic strawberries. I glanced at Ezra and shrugged. "Nothing."

Ezra winced. "I know I shouldn't be rooting for him to be our bad guy, but there is something about Forester that makes me want to punch him in the face."

There was spirit gum next to a display box of mustaches and eyebrows. I unscrewed the cap and took a whiff. Alcohol was the dominant scent, but behind that was the stringent aroma of resin. I made a face. "That's potent..."

"You're a narc, Sonny," a man says. He is wearing a double-breasted suit, and his dark hair is short and slicked back. "I'm gonna have to make an example out of you." He has a slight accent, but I can't decipher its origin.

"Please," another guy begs. "We're family." He's wearing a suit as well. Single-button coat. Pleated pants. Skinny tie. He's being held by two other men, both large. One of them is overweight and bald. Both are wearing black pants and white shirts. The muscle, for sure. The guy in trouble continues to plead, "You don't want to do this. Think of my wife. Your daughter. She'll never forgive you."

"She'll get over it." He takes a knife from his pocket and strolls over to his captive. "She's strong...like her pops." On that note, he strikes swift and without mercy, sinking the knife into the other man's chest. Blood oozes from the wound after he yanks out the blade. "Go," he says to his men. "Time to take out the trash."

"Whoa, Nora," Ezra said. "What is it?" He was holding me up. "What did you see?"

"I..." I shook my head to clear it. "I think you were right about the older guy, Forester. He killed his son-in-law." I met Ezra's gaze. "And...he enjoyed it."

CHAPTER
TWELVE

"You saw him kill someone?" Ezra's fists tightened at his side. "Are you sure? I mean, are you sure it was Forester?"

I shook my head. "You know how it is. I don't see faces, but this is his station. I mean," I plucked the Crockett wig from the Styrofoam head, "this belongs to him."

"You couldn't identify his voice?"

"You've heard how good he is at changing the way his voice sounds." I frowned. "I can't be sure."

"Damn it." Ezra let out a frustrated growl. "I knew there was something bad about that guy."

I put my hand on his back. "If he killed someone, you'll get him," I said.

"Did you get a sense that he had anything to do with the current murder plot?"

I tried to remember everything that was said, but none of it fit with the woman and her lover. I rubbed my temples to ward off a burgeoning headache. "I don't think so."

He put his arms around me. "Are you okay? You don't usually have so many visions in the short span of a few hours."

"They've been intense," I admitted. "The emotions behind the memories are abnormally heightened."

"Extreme, huh?" he rubbed my back.

I leaned my forehead against his chest. "Soul-crushing." My pity party ended when I heard the clickity-clack of heels in the hall. "Someone's coming," I hissed.

Ezra nodded and gestured for me to get behind the door. He did a quick search of the room and found a heavy-duty flashlight. He tapped the weighted end against his palm as if to test it, then got in front of me behind the door. He held up the flashlight, ready to defend us if needed.

"It's probably just one of the actors. Not our would-be killer. Try not to give anyone a concussion."

The corner of his mouth quirked up in a half-smile. "I'll try to control myself."

The clickity-clack got louder. "It has to be the woman playing Ms. Nelson."

"What makes you think that?"

"The two cheerleaders are wearing rubber-soled sneakers." I pointed to my low-tops. "I'm pretty sure this is just the male actors' room, so maybe she won't come in here."

Ezra turned to face me. "I guess we'll have to find something to do while we wait her out then."

"You're terrible," I said without any conviction. The way he gazed down at me with his bright green eyes made my stomach jittery. I licked my suddenly dry lips. "I think your beard is growing on me."

He gave it a light stroke, a cute smirk tugging at his lips.

The sound of high heels began to fade. I wanted to kiss his kissable lips, but a cooler head prevailed. "We better do what we came here to do before someone else comes along."

"I'm all for doing what we got to do," he said quietly. He leaned close and inhaled. A soft chuckle followed. "That's a lot of hair spray."

"As long as no one lights a match, we're safe." I rose up on my tiptoes and risked a kiss. The light brush of Ezra's lips, juxtaposed against the rough bristle of his beard, sent a tingle of excitement through me. I knew it wasn't safe to linger, but everything felt right when he held me in his arms. His fingertips slid over my waist and down my hips.

Ezra nuzzled my neck. "I can't wait to get this dress off you. The things I plan to do to you..."

"Oh, yeah?" I ran my fingers over the nape of his neck, tickling the small hairs. "Tell me more."

He raised and lowered his brows and narrowed his gaze on me. "I'd rather show you."

The return of the clickity-clacking made me inwardly groan. I shook my head. "Save that thought for later," I whispered. "You should probably turn around just in case you do have to bash someone."

"Or we could just make out until whoever it is passes by, or we get caught."

The sound of the sharp heels got louder again. "What is she doing out there?"

Ezra gave a slight head shake. "Maybe she's going back to the gym." He looked at his watch. "It's getting close to the end of the night. They're probably going to do a final closing act."

"Makes sense." I swallowed the lump in my throat. "This is just the first night. Maybe the plan for the accidentally on-purpose death is not happening until tomorrow sometime."

"I hope you're right." His gaze softened. "But

remember, you're not responsible if something happens."

"I know in here." I pointed to my head. "My heart is another story."

"It's a great heart." He placed his hand over the left side of my chest. "The best."

I held my breath as the clacking sounds got even louder then stopped abruptly right outside the room. Ezra turned his back to me and raised his guard again.

"Hello," a woman sang. "Nora. Are you back here?"

I bit back a curse. Daffney Graves. Ugh.

"I saw you come back here," Daffney said. "I hope I'm not interrupting...uhm, you know, anything important."

I put my hand over Ezra's—the one holding the flashlight-turned-weapon. Brain-panning the woman was mighty tempting. Ezra reached across himself with his other hand and patted mine.

"Nora," she called out.

Unfortunately, she was not going away. I made the executive decision to out us. After all, we'd already been caught in clinches several times during the evening. It wouldn't be a huge stretch for any of these strangers to believe that Ezra and I liked to love dangerously. I moved to Ezra's side and took his free hand. He gave me an affirmative nod.

"I'm here," I said as we skirted the door and walked out into the hallway. Daffney looked both pleased and scandalized.

"I saw you two make your escape from the gym. What are you doing?" she asked.

"Getting a little quiet time," I answered.

She smirked. "Sure. Quiet time."

I didn't like her tone. "We better get back." I forced a smile. "Don't want to get sent to the principal's office for getting caught without a hall pass."

"Can we talk for a minute?" Daffney's gaze flicked to Ezra then back to me. "Alone," she added.

"Uhm..."

Ezra's grip on my hand tightened. "Can't right now," he said abruptly. "We have to go." He led me out the door away from the Graves sister.

I gave him a questioning look.

"I find her highly suspicious," he said quickly. "That's twice now she's asked to speak to you alone. Made a point about wanting you away from me. That's not happening."

"You don't think..."

"I don't even care. I'm not risking you," he said.

We promised to stay in pairs, so I didn't disagree with him. However, I hadn't seen Daffney as anything more than a harmless nuisance. Did I need to reevaluate my opinion of my old sorority sister? As we rounded the corner to the hall that led back to the gym, the lights flickered on again.

"What are you two doing back here?" Tim Dean, still sporting his A Flock of Seagulls hairstyle, stood in the center of the hall. He crossed his arms over his chest. "You have your own private room in the guest wing. If you can't follow the rules of the event, then I'll have to ask you to leave."

Ezra draped his arm over my shoulders. "It's hard not to relive a few high school fantasies." He glanced down at me and winked before turning his gaze back to Tim. "You understand, right?"

Tim's stern stare eased. "Actually, I do. I had a few hot-for-teacher fantasies in my younger days." He shook his head. "But I still can't let you break the rules." He jerked his thumb toward the door. "Out."

Tim was on my list as a potential victim. I decided to risk getting nosy to find out if he was even a viable candidate. "Hey," I asked as we headed past Tim. "Are you and the cute blonde cheerleader married?" They'd sounded cozy in the kitchen.

His chin jerked down to his chest. "Yes, actually." His gaze narrowed at me, but he was smiling. "Just last year."

"Congratulations," Ezra told him.

"Oh, how long have you guys been together?"

He paused for a moment, then answered, "A few years, but it took me a little bit to convince her to say yes. Lynn..." He frowned. "She's special."

"I'm sure she is." I looped my arm in Ezra's. "We'll get out of your hair."

"And you'll stay out of the staff areas?" He made it a question.

"Yep," I said. "Absolutely."

A loud *pop* and a scream brought us all up short. Ezra grabbed Tim by the arm. "Is this part of the mystery?"

"No," Tim groaned.

"Daffney," I said. "We left her in the dressing room." I took off after Ezra, but I wasn't nearly as fast. He was already in the room before I was barely around the corner. A cloud of white haze billowed from the room.

Tim followed us down the hall.

When we got to the door, Daffney was on the ground, her face bleeding, and glass was everywhere. Ezra was next to her, his fingers touching her neck. "She has a pulse," he said. "We need to call an ambulance." When I tried to come in, he held up his hand. There was a burn on it. "Stay back, Nora. There's glass everywhere, and it has a corrosive agent on it."

Tim looked grim as he pulled out his phone. "Why was she in here? Why are any of you back here? This isn't—" He cursed under his breath. "This is not how this weekend was supposed to go."

"Do you smell that?" The crisp scent of ozone reached me out in the hall. "What is that?"

"I'm sorry," a woman says. Her face is a blur, as faces always are in my visions, but I can vaguely make out the surroundings. The room is familiar. The furniture is different, but I recognized the windows and the view of the courtyard. This is the math room. Only, it has stations with sinks.

"I should've never let it get this far. It's wrong," a woman says. "It can cost me everything if we get caught. It has to be over."

A guy grabs her and tries to pull her into his arms, but she jerks away from him.

"Don't, Juliet. You know I love you," he replies. He's got short dark hair, and he's wearing jeans and a t-shirt, but in the dim light, I can't make out the color. The desperation in his tone sends a pang of pity through me. His voice breaks, "I don't want to live without you."

"Romeo," she says solemnly, "With love's light wings do I perch these walls,

For stony limits cannot hold love out." She kisses him. "I want to be with you more than anything. But there's only one way to make that happen."

He sounds young, like my godson Marco's age. His words are full of anguish. "I don't know if I can do it." He shakes his head. "I don't know if I can kill him."

As I come out of the vision, I couldn't shake the torment I'd felt just seconds earlier. There'd been such a sense of desperation along with a fear of loss. He wanted to please her, to make her stay, but he was also very afraid. The memory had been like the one I'd had earlier with the Winnie-the-Pooh references, but this one had gone all Shakespearean. Was I watching history repeat itself?

Or had Romeo and Juliet waited decades to put their plan into motion?

CHAPTER
THIRTEEN

"Nora," Ezra said as I braced myself against the door. "You okay?" His eyes were shadowed with worry.

I nodded. "Just another..." I glanced at Tim. "Headache," I said. "How's Daffney?"

"Pulse is thready. She's losing a lot of blood."

"I can't get a signal back here. This school has always had terrible reception," Tim said. "I'm going to have to go outside."

"The glass might've nicked an artery." I turned to Tim. "We can help her now, if you'll just go get Scott Graham."

"The gym is full of people, and what if he's not in there now?" Tim asked. "It'll be quicker if you help me find him." He bit down on his lower lip. "This is bad."

I caught Ezra's eye. His expression was wary, but he nodded. I put my hand on Tim's shoulder. "We're going to help her. I'll find the doc. You get outside to make your call."

Tim let out a slow, measured breath then nodded curtly. "That's a good plan."

We took the front hall that crossed the library and the office. Lynn and Sawyer were striding up the hall toward us.

"Are you okay?" Lynn asked Tim. "We heard a scream. Tony and Tina are searching the kitchen, Forester..." She grimaced. "He's finding his center, apparently. Do you know what happened?" She clutched her sweater at the chest. "I was so worried, baby."

"Some glass broke in the dressing room. One of the guests was in there when it happened. I have to call an ambulance."

Sawyer's expression hardened. "Can I help?" His gaze was narrowed on Tim.

"You can help us find Nora's friend. A doctor," Tim said.

"Scott Graham," I added. "He's with a woman named Gilly Martin."

"I'll go check on the guest," Lynn said. "Which one was it?"

"Daffney Graves," I told her. "Someone needs to let her sister know what's happening."

"I can do that." Sawyer, who was dressed as Biff the Stiff, pursed his lips in a deep frown. "The woman, uh, made a pass at me earlier. I know exactly who she is."

He turned away—and that's when I noticed the umbrella pin on his collar.

Pooh. Honeybees. And Christopher Robin was always carrying an umbrella. While I wasn't an expert on all things Pooh-related like Nellie Lox, the books and the movies had been around since I was a kid.

Looking at the two of them, I knew I'd found my would-be killers.

Lynn was an attractive woman in her forties, she looked to be a few years older than her husband, and about fifteen to twenty years older than Sawyer. I wasn't judging. I was in love with a man who was a lot younger than me. However, Ezra and I weren't plotting murder.

First priority was saving Daffney, but that didn't mean I couldn't warn Tim about his wife and her young lover.

"We should go. Daffney needs medical attention like right now." I touched Tim's arm. "Let's go." Sawyer and Lynn parted ways. Sawyer to the gym, and Lynn rushed down the hall to the dressing room.

After they were gone, I glanced around to make sure no one was in earshot. I wasn't sure how to tell him that his wife was looking to become a widow, so I went for the rip-the-Band-Aid-off method of bad news. "Tim...I...I think you're in danger. I think that explosion was meant for you."

"What makes you think that?"

Now, it was time to sell the lie. "I overheard her talking with someone. I think that Buzz guy. She called him Romeo...and Christopher. Code names, I think. They were plotting to kill her husband. You." I gave him a sympathetic look. "We need to ask for the police when you call for the ambulance. You are in very real danger."

He had a hold of my upper arm. I thought he was leading me outside, but his grip tightened. Before we could head to the school entrance, he yanked me sideways and pulled me into the front office. Before I could react, he shoved me farther into the interior of the room and locked the bolt on the door behind us.

"Tim? I know this is a shock..." I scrambled backward until my shoulder bumped a wall. In the vision, the woman had acted scared. Cripes, had I just spent the entire evening trying to save a man who abused his wife? "We should go outside," I said with as much calm as I could muster. "Ezra, my boyfriend, he's a cop. He'll be worried about me. Right now, this is a misunderstanding. Let's keep it that way."

Tim grabbed a stone paperweight from the counter. "I'm not Lynn's first husband," he said, his voice robotic as if he were in shock. "I..." He shook his head. "Her first husband is dead." He took a menacing step forward, his fingers going white as he clenched the paperweight in his right hand. "I was a senior in high school at the time." A slight smile turned up his lips. "A bit of a nerd really. But Lynn, she knows how to make you feel special." His brow furrowed. "Her light shines so bright." His eyes glazed as he stared off. "But soft, what light through yonder window breaks? It is the East, and Juliet is the sun." A soft chuckle rose in his throat. "She was my sun."

Oh, God. She had been his teacher. He'd been a high school student who'd been manipulated by a woman who should've known better. I felt along the wall for anything I could use in my defense as I stalled for time. "You're Romeo," I said. "You loved her."

His glassy-eyed wet glare met my gaze. "I still love her."

"She wants you dead, Romeo."

"If that's my fate, so be it," he said. "I killed for her. It's not a stretch to die for her."

"That's exactly what she wants." My fingers landed on a plug in a wall socket. The cord was thick and round, like an extension cord, but I didn't dare look to see what was attached to the other end. I wasn't about to take my eyes off Tim.

"She loves me," he said. "She just..." He gave a slight headshake as if trying to discard whatever he was going to say.

"You were always doomed, right?" I asked. "Romeo and Juliet. The classic star-crossed lovers." The metaphor for which I understood when it came to Tim and Lynn, but I struggled to understand the Winnie-the-Pooh thing. "That's why she's moved on."

He kicked a nearby waste basket at me. I let out a surprised shout as the contents, shredded paper mostly, rained down on me like confetti.

I waited a second to see if he was going to do anything else, then asked, "Why Romeo?"

"I was the lead in our school play my senior year. Lynn was the drama teacher. I played sports but I was always in trouble. She helped me grow up."

Faster than you should've, I thought with disgust. "You didn't want to do it," I said, remembering the scared, conflicted teenager in my vision. "You knew it was wrong."

"He abused her. Physically. Mentally. Emotionally. She had to be freed from him." He pressed the base of his palm over his eye. "I did what I had to do to be the man she needed."

"But you were a boy." I couldn't imagine how they managed to stay together all these years. He still seemed like a reluctant killer. "How old are you now?"

"Old enough to not fall for any tricks."

"I mean, how long ago were you a senior? When did you start—" I carefully chose my next words. He was abused by a person who held power over him, but I didn't want to trigger his rage again. "How long ago did you fall in love?"

"Fifteen years," Tim answered.

"How did you manage to stay together after..."

He smiled but his eyes were sad. "I kept my distance. I went to college, got my degree in education and science, then came back to Button Falls to teach. It didn't take much to start back up where we left off." His eyes grew distant. "She was reluctant at first, but I knew she still loved me."

He'd been a science teacher at this school. I remembered the coffee mug. HG, the symbol for mercury, had been on the middle table. The first table had held the exploding glass water bottle that had injured Daffney. Oh, gawd.

"When did you know Lynn was having an affair?"

Tim's expression turned stark. "When that... boy," he spat out the word, "started wearing the cologne she loves so much." His hand holding the paperweight shook as he fixed his stare on me. "It's her favorite. It was her father's, and she said it made her feel safe. Made her feel loved. Her mother was insane."

Like mother like daughter, I thought. I thought about the child and the mother in my vision. It had to have been Lynn with her mother. "The cologne," I said. "Is it Drakkar Noir?"

Tim had a faraway expression on his face. "She said the cologne was the only thing she had left of her parents." He chuckled without real humor. "Winnie-the-Pooh. Of course," he said. "That was the play where I'm sure Lynne made Sawyer her young protégé." Tim blinked at me. "He played Christopher Robin. Do you know why Christopher needed Pooh?" he asked me.

I shook my head and gently curled my fingers around the electric cord, hoping it wasn't connected to a fridge or some other immovable object. If I could surprise Tim, I had a chance of making it to the door.

"Because the boy was lonely. He had no one. His mother was gone. His father worked all the time. His only companion was a stuffed bear." Tears crested his eyes. "That's what she does. She sees the loneliness inside you. And when she's with you, you feel like you'll never be lonely again."

Cripes, why had I left Ezra? We should've stuck to the plan of two by two, but a woman's life was in danger. I mentally smacked myself. Now there were two women's lives in danger. "How old is Sawyer?"

Tim rolled his eyes. "I don't know. Twenty." He scowled. "Maybe. Lynn likes them young."

I had to keep him talking. Talking was better than hitting. "You knew they were trying to kill you," I told him. "Your wife and the young man."

He nodded. "It wasn't hard to figure out. But that kid isn't very smart."

"How did you turn his water bottle into an explosive? What science experiment?"

"Some sodium metal shavings in the straw spout. Open it up, the metal drops into the water. Exothermic reaction goes boom." He made an exploding gesture with his free hand. "I didn't expect that nosy bitch to ruin my plans. If she'd left it alone, it would be Sawyer on the ground back there. Not her." He squinted his eyes on me. "What am I going to do with you?"

"You could let me go," I said helpfully.

He stalked toward me, his hand raised above his head. "I'm sorry, Nora. I'm afraid that's not an option."

Well, crap.

CHAPTER
FOURTEEN

"You don't want to do this, Tim. Lynn isn't worth a first-degree murder charge. She's cheating on you." These were things he already knew, but unfortunately, the woman must've had a magic vagina, because Tim didn't blame her. He blamed Sawyer and himself, and he didn't care that his black widow wife was the biggest culprit of all.

"We were trying to call from the office phone, and you tripped and hit your head," he said as he moved closer. "You've been a bit wobbly tonight. I mean, you nearly passed out in the hall. It will be a tragedy." He sounded disconnected from his emotions, and insidious fear coiled in my gut.

"They won't believe you, Tim. You won't get away with it."

He smiled. "I got away with it for twelve years. I like my chances."

Crap. Crap. Crap.

I yanked on the cord. A space heater sitting on top of a file cabinet clambered to the floor. The front grate busted away from the appliance and skid across the tile. Tim barked a sound of surprise and jumped sideways as I yanked the cord again, and the heater smashed against the cabinet and made an impressively loud bang.

Adrenaline gave me wings, and I flew to the door. Before I could rotate the slide bolt, Tim had his hand on my sleeve. He yanked me hard. I yelped as my dress tore, and I stumbled sideways into the office window. I pushed the blinds aside and could see guests in the corridor, including an angelic vision in a ruched red dress. "Gilly!" I bellowed. "Gilly in here!" I banged on the glass. "Help!"

She looked in my direction, but Tim grabbed me, and the blinds closed. He swung the paperweight at me, and I ducked.

I'd grown up as a cop's daughter, I'd been a cop's wife, and I was now dating another cop. I'd picked up some self-defense moves over the years. When Tim swung on me again, I rotated into the blow and swung my elbow around to smash him in the face. It hurt both of us when the strike landed. I followed with a stomp on his arch, wishing like hell I'd worn hard-soled boots instead of sneakers.

There was pounding on the door as I dropped down to the ground and rolled away from Tim. "You hear that, you son-of-a-bitch? They're coming. They're coming for you. No more getting away with it." I panted with effort as I got to my knees.

"I'm gonna kill you," he seethed. He rushed at me, and when he raised his hand to pummel me, I punched out with all my might, and nailed him in his family jewels.

Tim howled as he doubled over and dropped the stone paperweight. I picked it up before he could and smacked him across the temple with it, sending him all the way to the floor. The unconscious bastard landed across my lap. I kicked him off me and crawled to the door. I used the handle to pull myself to a stand, then unlocked the door.

Gilly was the first to rush in. "Nora!" Her horrified, worried expression told me all I needed to know.

I hugged her tightly as she wrapped her arms around me.

"Cripes, you had me so scared," she said. "We couldn't get in. That door had to be designed for war."

"Nora!" Pippa exclaimed as she joined in on the hug.

Jordy rushed past us, grabbed the cord I'd used to save my life, and hog-tied Tim Dean.

"You hurt?" Pippa asked me.

"Nothing but my pride." I'd really thought Tim had been the injured party in this plot. Turned out, he was a killer, and he'd been prepared to kill again. "Thanks to my heroes," I told her.

Gilly leaned back and glanced at the knocked-out, tied-up bad guy on the ground. "Babe, you're your own hero."

"You found me. That made all the difference. If you hadn't seen me," I said, my voice and body shaky now that the adrenaline had worn off. "It could've ended differently."

"But it didn't." She gave my back a brisk rub.

"Ezra needs us," I said. "He has Daffney."

"I know," she told me. "That Biff guy found us. He sent Scott down there."

"An ambulance?"

"Tony Morton called. He said his phone had all the bars, and when we couldn't find you…" She made a fist and shook it in Tim's direction. "Is it bad to kick a guy when he's down?"

I cracked a smile. "He'll get his due in prison."

"I'll go check on Ezra and Scott," Jordy said. "Are

you guys all right here?"

I nodded. "Tell Ezra what happened. Tell him I'm okay."

"I will," he said.

Morton came into the office after Jordy departed. "The police and an ambulance are on the way." His eyes widened as he took in the prone figure of Tim Dean. "He was always such a quiet man."

"It's always the quiet ones," Gilly said solemnly.

Tim groaned and began to stir.

Gilly looked at me. "Are you sure I can't kick him?"

"It would, like, be, like, a rad move against a really bad dude," Pippa said.

Gilly snickered. "He's totally grody to the max."

My heart filled with love for my two friends who always had my back no matter what. "You guys are totally bitchin' besties." I glanced down at Tim then back to Gilly. "Do you want to make a citizen's arrest? I think Ezra promised you that."

She grinned. "I absolutely do." She walked over to Tim, toed him with the end of her shoe, then balled her fists on her hips. "Okay, dirtbag, you have the right to remain silent." She glanced back at me. "Maybe I should wait until he's awake."

I crinkled my nose at her. "However you want to

play it. It's your birthday, after all."

I'D NEVER BEEN SO grateful when the ambulance and the police showed up. The police arrested Tim Dean, and after I gave them my statement, they took Lynn Gleason and Sawyer Johnson in for questioning. I had a feeling Tim was going to give them an earful about his wife and her lover. I hoped all three got their just dues.

The paramedics had gotten Daffney's bleeding stopped and had hooked her up to an IV. They looked at me, but other than a few bumps and bruises, I was fine. Ezra, however, had needed to be treated for minor burns. Velma had already headed to the hospital in her own car. I stood with Ezra as they loaded Daffney into the ambulance. She refused to look in Ezra's direction.

"You saved her life," I said. "Why is she acting like she'll turn to stone if she captures your eye?"

He chuckled. "She propositioned me."

My eyes widened as I realized what he said. "She what?"

"After you left the room with Dean, she came around. She asked me how much I cost."

"I don't understand."

He grinned. "She thought I was a prostitute, Nora. She wanted to know how much I charged for my services."

I couldn't hide my shock. "No."

"Yep." He raised his brows in amusement. "Imagine her surprise when I told her I was a cop."

"I can imagine." I turned to face him. "This means..." I put my fingers over my mouth. "Oh, my gawd. She thought I'd hired you to be my date."

He laughed out loud at that. "Yep."

"And what did you tell her?"

"I told her that I'd never loved anyone the way I love you, and that I've never been loved better by anyone before you." He took me in his arms. "I'm so happy you didn't get hurt."

"Me too," I said. I kissed him.

"Excuse me," a man interrupted. "What is going on?"

I looked over my shoulder to see Robert Forester standing behind me. Ezra practically vibrated.

"You," he said, his voice full of accusation.

I'd nearly forgotten about the vision I'd had when the man had crossed paths with me earlier. I stepped away from Ezra as he quickly moved around me, grabbed Forester and shoved him against the side of the ambulance. "You're under arrest," he said.

"For what?" the actor sputtered. "I haven't done anything." He'd lost his upper-crust accent, and it had been replaced with something that sounded more like he'd come from the south.

"You killed a man," I said. "You stabbed him with a knife."

"I never!" he exclaimed.

"Sonny," I told him. "Does that ring any bells?"

He coughed. "Sonny. You mean, Sonny Carolla?"

"Maybe," I admitted. There'd been no last names in my vision.

"Carolla?" Ezra asked.

"What? Have you heard of Sonny Carolla?" I asked Ezra.

"Millions of people have heard of Sonny Carolla," the actor sputtered.

"Oh my." I let out a slow breath to still my excitement. Had I just broken some great unsolved case? A zing of thrill zipped through me as I imagined his poster coming down from the FBI's most wanted billboard.

Ezra looked flummoxed as he eased his hold on the older man. "Uhm, I'm afraid there's been a mistake."

"I'll say." Forester took a few steps away. "I'll never get away from Victor Patrone."

"Victor Patrone?" Was Forester in hiding from

another bad guy?

Ezra frowned and shook his head. "I don't think we need to—"

The actor snarled. "That character ruined my life." He raised his fist and shook it. "Do you know how many death threats I got daily from disgruntled housewives who wanted to kill me for executing their favorite character?"

"Favorite character? I'm really confused," I said. I looked to Ezra for answers.

He gave me a half-grimace, half-smile. "*As The Globe Burns*," he said. "It was a soap opera in the nineties." He gave Forester an apologetic shrug. "I'm afraid my mom was one of those angry fans." He softly laughed. "Damn, I forgot all about that. She punched a wall when you killed off Sonny."

"Young man," Forester said, straightening his jacket and adjusting his dignity. "I didn't kill him off. The writers did. If you want to manhandle someone, I will happily give you their names."

"Nope. All good." Ezra tilted his head and gave the man a tight-lipped smile. "Again, I apologize."

Before Forester could walk away, I asked him, "Why are you wearing that cologne?" Surely, not all the straight guys were sleeping with Lynn.

The older man, still acting wounded and offended, sniffed his displeasure. "It was...available." Ah, he'd used either Tim's or Sawyer's cologne. That made more sense as to why I was getting hits of them off Forester. The actor yanked his collar up. "Now, if you'll excuse me, I need to go meditate...again." I couldn't blame him for wanting to find his Zen again. He'd been taken to task over an almost thirty-year-old grudge.

I wrapped my arms around Ezra's waist. "Your mom used to watch, huh?"

He kissed my forehead. "I might've caught a few episodes here or there."

"Only a few?" I grinned and slid my hand up the back of his shirt.

He stiffened at my cold fingers against his skin. "We don't need to tell the others about this, er, misunderstanding, do we?"

"It'll be our little secret," I told him. "How about we get the gang and pack it in? I think this murder mystery weekend is a bust, and I'm ready to go home and get in my own bed..." I kissed him again. "With you."

"That sounds like an event I can get into." He nipped my lower lip. "Admission free."

"You're so bad."

He reached down and cupped my butt with both hands. "I'm ready to show you just how bad I can be."

"Excuse me," Gilly said. She was standing with Scott, Pippa, and Jordy. "I figured out who the killer is. You know, the one who killed Biff the jock." She arched her brow and with her best detective voice, she said, "The murderer is Leah Standish."

"Ironic," Pippa said. "You know, since she orchestrated the death of one husband and was trying to off another."

Gilly gave her a don't-ruin-my-moment stare. With a lot of enthusiasm, she said, "From the clues, I deduced that Leah was in love with Mr. Moore, who had stopped seeing her when Biff blackmailed him. Moore broke up with Leah, so she caused trouble between Mary Jane Masterson, Brian Bender, and Biff. It was her way of throwing suspicion away from herself. She hit him with a trophy that was hidden in one of the rooms and strangled him with a rope covered in chemical powder to get revenge on the teacher who dumped her to save his job!" She smacked the bottom of her fist against her palm. "Boom! Birthday girl gets bragging rights."

"Okay," I said. "Congratulations. I mean, I solved a real crime, but sure, I'll give you this one."

Pippa rolled her eyes. "Is it really fair to say Gilly solved the fake case if Tony Morton told her the solution."

Gilly backhanded Pippa's arm. "Spoilsport."

Gilly looked around. "I hope Tony and Tina, who I found out are total BFFs since college and partners in *School's Out for Murder,* keep the event going. They said they had full bookings clear through to the fall. They'll just need to find a couple of actors..." She turned her eager stare at me.

"Have fun with that," I snorted.

"I'm tempted," Gilly said. "Especially with the twins off to college. But I probably won't. I need another full-time job like I need another hole in my head." She sighed. "Ah well, let's get our crap and get the heck out of here. We can eat birthday cake at my house tomorrow."

Scott put his arm around her from behind. "Cake is always a reason to celebrate."

"Yeah," I agreed. I glanced around at my circle of friends, feeling damn lucky to have them in my life. My besties had fought to try and save me, the same as I would do for them. I nodded to Gilly. "And as far as I'm concerned, you get total bragging rights."

"Good," she said. She took a large metal button from her pocket and put it on her coat. "Because I have the super sleuth badge, and I plan to wear it with pride."

"As you should." I laughed. "Happy birthday, super sleuth."

CHAPTER
FIFTEEN

A *few weeks later...*
We'd had a super slow day at Scents & Scentsability and decided to close early. Ezra had called earlier in the day and told me he had some news he said he wanted to tell me in person. So, closing early worked for me. It would give me time to shave my legs and chill a bottle of wine before Ezra got to my place.

Halfway through our final clean up and front of house inventory, Gilly had gotten a call. She'd taken her phone back to her massage room and closed the door. The pitch of her voice, even though we couldn't make out the words, ranged from surprised to excited.

"Who is she talking to?" I asked Pippa.

Pippa shrugged. "Maybe Scott." A blond lock of

hair escaped her ponytail, and she tucked it behind her ear.

"The two of them are really great together," I said.

Pippa smiled. "They're so adorable."

Scott had confessed his love to Gilly at the Murder High, and she'd been walking on cloud nine since. I was ecstatic she finally found a guy who treated her with kindness and respect, and the sizzling chemistry between them was undeniable. "Maybe they're having phone sex," I teased.

Pippa appeared satisfyingly scandalized. "No," she said. "She wouldn't...."

I shrugged. "Wouldn't she?" I grabbed a box of lavender and bergamot pillow spray. Lavender was great for sleep and headaches, and the bergamot added a warm note of citrus that aided in relaxation. I had several customers who tended to buy out my supplies monthly.

A peel of laughter from the spa area made us both raise our brows.

"I've never laughed that hard when it comes to sex," I commented

"Yeah," Pippa agreed. "That kind of laughing is usually a boner killer."

I choked. "Talking from experience, huh?"

She grinned and shook her head. "Not recent experience."

I finished restocking sprays. "I'm sure Jordy's glad to hear that."

"Har har," Pippa countered.

"I'm so glad you called," Gilly said as she came around the corner from the massage. She had a grin on her face that brightened her brown eyes. "I'm looking forward to Monday." She gave Pippa and me a quick nod. "All right," she finished up. "I'll see you soon." She took the phone away from her ear and tapped the screen. After a brief pause, she turned to us and squealed. "I'm going to be an actor!"

"What in the world?" Pippa asked.

"School's Out For Murder, Incorporated," she said as an explanation. "That was Tony Morton. We've been texting since that weekend. He and Tina are going to continue the business."

"That's great," I said. "I'm glad they aren't giving up on their dream."

Ezra had been tracking the progress on the investigation. He'd told me a few days ago that Tim Dean confessed to killing Leah's first husband when he was her student, and he's willing to testify that she coerced him. Apparently, she was pulling the same game on Sawyer that she had Tim. I shivered just thinking about

Leah's twisted mind. Both men in her life had been vulnerable, and she'd taken advantage of her position over them. Her relationships with both of them were more about power than anything close to love.

"And they want you to be one of the actors?" Pippa asked.

Gilly's shoulders practically raised to her ears as she nodded. "Tony asked me if I wanted a part."

"And you said yes?" Pippa frowned, and I could see the worry on her face. "What about your clients?"

"It's only a trial run," Gilly said. "And I only have to go over to Button Falls a couple of times a week, and then on weekends."

Gilly sounded enthusiastic about the prospect of acting. Maybe it was the idea of doing something new with her life, and why shouldn't she? After all, I'd started over, and that hadn't turned out bad at all.

"Cool," I said to her. "It sounds like a lot of fun."

"What about Scott?" Pippa asked. "It's going to cut down on the time you get to spend with him."

Ezra had been gone undercover for a few weeks, and I'd missed him to the extreme. Even so, I'd have never stood in his way.

Gilly put her hand on Pippa's and gave it a squeeze. "I'm not going to live my life trying to please someone else, especially if it means I have to give up a little of my own happiness." She smiled. "Not anymore. I love him, and I don't want to lose him," she said. "But I'm not going to make decisions out of fear."

I studied my BFF for a moment, amazed at her strength and conviction. She was choosing herself for the first time ever, and I was completely on board for it. "I see a lot of trips to Button Falls in the good doctor's future."

She gave me a hopeful smile. "I'll have my own private room."

"I guess there's only one thing to say." Pippa glanced at me, and I caught her meaning.

In unison, we both said, "Break a leg."

Gilly's lower lip jutted in a cute pout. "You guuuys." She held out her arms. "Group hug."

She didn't have to ask us twice as we all huddled in.

Later that evening...

After the buzzing stopped, the resulting silence only increased my anticipation. "Come on," I whined. My impatience was getting the better of me. "I want to see."

I heard a chuckle from the bathroom, and a tremor of excitement ran through me.

Ezra, without fanfare, walked into the bedroom, patting his face with a towel. When he took the towel away, his clean-shaven appearance stole my breath.

I gave a slow whistle and he rewarded me with a smile. It was the first time since his return home that I'd seen his cute dimples. He rubbed his angular, kissable jaw with the back of his fingers, and asked, "Better?"

"God, I've missed that face," I replied. The news was that he'd finally been given the greenlight from the taskforce commander that he could ditch the face-fur. I'd insisted on making it an event.

Ezra knelt on the floor in front of me and nudged his hips between my knees. He kissed my neck. "How much did you miss this face?"

I giggled. "Put it this way, I won't miss the beard burn on more sensitive areas."

Ezra grinned at me and waggled his brow. "I think we should take the new face for a test drive."

"I love a good joy ride."

He slid his arms around my waist as he got to his feet. I squealed with delight as he lifted me farther onto the bed. "Buckle up." His lips pressed against mine as he finished with, "It's going to be a bumpy ride."

I slung my arms around his neck and laughed. This. The two of us together. I couldn't remember ever being so happy.

The End...for now

EARTH SPELLS ARE EASY
GRIMOIRES OF A MIDDLE-AGED WITCH
BOOK 1

As a forty-three-year-old, newly divorced, single mom, I know two things for certain, starting over sucks, and magic isn't real. At least that's

what I thought. I mean, starting over really does stink, but when it comes to magic, I have to rethink everything.

I've spent the last year since my ex left me going through the motions. Get up. Work. Care for a grumpy teenager. Cook dinner. Go to bed. Wash. Rinse. Repeat.

Nothing changes… Until it does.

After bidding on a box of old books at an estate auction, I'm experiencing changes.

And I'm not talking about menopause.

My garden gnome Linda has come to life. No, really. Her name is Linda, and she never shuts up. A chonky cat with a few secrets of his own has adopted me. And a gorgeous professor of the occult tells me I'm a witch.

Right now, I'm not sure who's crazier—me, Linda or the hottie professor.

If this is my new reality, it's nature's cruel midlife trick. I'm learning fast that earth spells might be easy, but they aren't cheap. All magic exacts a toll, and if I don't master the elements, the elements will be the death of me.

Literally.

Chapter One

The garlicky scent of take-out created a nauseating stench I found hard to ignore. Now, I would forever associate Mongolian Beef with divorce, and it made me want to yark.

I passed the legal documents across the kitchen table to my lawyer Donald Overton III then glanced around my kitchen. "Sorry about the mess, Don." There were two plates, silverware, and cups in the sink, and it had been the third time I'd said I was sorry since his arrival.

"The place is cleaner than my house," he said.

Don, who was a six-foot-four man with rounded shoulders and a big, balding head to match, wasn't just my lawyer. He was also my brother-in-law. Which meant I knew he was stretching the truth to spare my feelings. My sister Rose was a meticulous housekeeper. "Is that it?" I asked.

He gave me a sympathetic look, emphasis on the *pathetic*, and nodded. "That's it, Iris. Done is done."

I rubbed my face. "Done is done," I repeated. "I'm officially Iris Everlee." I'd legally changed it a few weeks earlier. Still, it hadn't felt definitive that I was no longer a Callahan until I'd signed the divorce papers.

I'd wasted eighteen years married to a man who left me for someone else. Someone younger.

Someone male. My ex, it turned out, was bisexual. I have always been open-minded. I genuinely believe, love is love and that people should live their truths. But when it's your husband, it's a lot harder to be congratulatory about someone discovering their "authentic self."

"Thanks for bringing those to me." I stood up from the table. "I have to get Michael up for practice."

Michael was my seventeen-year-old son. I worried he'd suffered the most during the divorce. But my son had always been a quiet child, not distant or anti-social, just even keel and low drama. It made it extremely difficult to gauge his real feelings most of the time.

"Is he still playing football?" Don asked.

"Yep. Today's the first day of spring training."

Don added, "You look like you need a friend. You should call Rose."

Unable to shake the feeling of trepidation, I said, "I'm fine. I'll be okay."

Don gave me a grim smile, then gathered up the paperwork and slipped it into a folder. "I'll get these filed at the courthouse today. You and Michael should come to dinner tomorrow night."

I stood up and walked him out of the kitchen

and through the living room to the front door. "I'll call Rose later. I promise," I told him, which had been the only promise Don had been trying to extract. Of course, I hadn't promised *when* I would call.

"Please do. You know how Rose gets." My brother-in-law gave me a gentle shoulder squeeze, then left.

I had three sisters and one brother. Rose, the youngest of us all, had taken on the responsibility as the family worrywart since our mother died of pancreatic cancer five years earlier. The doctors had given her three or four months to live, but she'd died three weeks later in her sleep because the cancer had strangled her aorta and caused an aneurysm.

I closed the door and made my way down the dark hallway past the kitchen. Even with the door closed, the foul scents of boy stink threatened to knock me off my feet. Garlic leftovers had nothing on *Ewwww de Son*. I tapped on the door. No response. I pounded my fist against the wood. Still no response.

I opened the door a crack. "Hello?" I leaned on the door to open it wider as the sickly sweet and sour odors hit me full force, burning the back of my nostrils.

My eyesight adjusted to the dark. I saw a small mountain of dirty clothes wedged behind the door, barring further entry. I could see long toes peeking over the edge of a queen-sized mattress. Otherwise, I wouldn't have known a human being occupied the bed.

"Michael, damn it." Lately, "damn it" had been his middle name. "Let me in."

"What do you want?" came his muffled voice full of sleepy annoyance.

"I want you to open this stupid door right now."

"Go away."

"I'll go away. I'll go away to the garage and get a screwdriver and a hammer and take this freaking door off its hinges." Screw this. I pushed the door as hard as I could. Mount Dirt & Grime slid across the carpet and allowed me entry.

His foot drifted out of sight. He was moving—another good sign.

"What the hell died in your room? It smells like a serial killer's drop zone."

The boy sat up, his short hair looking too perfect to be slept in, just like his father. He scratched his patchy goatee. "Dramatic much?" His voice, low and pleasant in tone, held an edge of sarcasm.

I fought back a smile. My kid was beautiful, no

doubt about it. He was one of the few things Evan and I had done right.

He blinked his soft brown eyes in my direction. "I'm not going to practice."

"Oh, you're going." I picked up a pair of sweatpants, a green pair at the top of the pile, and chucked them at him. "Get dressed."

He groaned and threw himself onto the bed, pulling the covers over his shoulders. "I'm tired."

"You wouldn't be so tired if you weren't up all night playing video games with your buddies."

He grunted. Translation: *Whatever.*

"Michael Evan Callahan, you will get yourself out of bed this minute. You promised your father."

He moaned his dissent. "Coach is going to be there," he replied.

"If you want a relationship with your dad, you're going to have to come to terms with the fact that Coach Adam is a part of his life now." I sounded so reasonable, even to my own ears. Inside, I was screaming. It had been a year since Evan and I had separated, and most of the time, I tried to not hate him for what he'd done to our family, but sometimes I struggled with taking the higher road.

"Yeah, well, you didn't catch them going at it." He was sitting up now, rubbing the sleep from his eyes. "And you expect me to come to terms with it."

Unfortunately, my son had discovered his father's infidelity before me. He'd gone to talk to Coach Adam after school hours and found him and Evan kissing in the coach's office. Michael had come home and locked himself in his bedroom that night. I could still see his hurt and rage. Being caught by our kid was what prompted Evan to finally come clean with me.

Sighing, I sat on the bed next to Michael and put my hand on his shoulder. "Kissing is not going at it," I said.

My oldest sister Dahlia was a family counselor. She'd recommended someone for the family to see, including Evan, in order for us to move forward with our lives.

"Close enough," he countered.

It took months for Michael to even look at his father, then a few months more for him to have a civil conversation with him. I was angry with Evan, but still, I was glad that Michael was finally seeing him again. They'd been taking it slowly. A few lunches and dinners here and there. One month ago, their relationship had taken another setback when Evan and Adam decided to go public and move in together.

I missed the days when I could scoop Michael into my arms and cuddle him. He was at that age now where he would have pulled away if I tried to comfort him. As it was, I could feel him shrink at my consoling touch. How could I expect him to understand and accept his father's new life when I could hardly think about him without my own rage clouding my mind? I felt like I'd wasted my best years on him. He'd promised to love me until *death do we part*. Yes, I lost my husband, but I'd also lost my best friend. Evan and I had more in common than anyone I'd ever met. We had the same tastes in books, music, and movies. We'd shared similar political and philosophical beliefs, and we'd rarely ran out of conversation.

On top of that, our sex life had been good. Don't get me wrong, we'd had our share of arguments. It's hard to be with someone for eighteen years and not have any fights, but we'd always made up. In other words, his falling in love with someone else, regardless of gender, had been a complete blindside.

"Michael," I said, my voice gentle but strained. "I understand that you're uncomfortable around your dad and Adam but avoiding them is not going to make your life any better or easier. Do you want a relationship with your father?"

The teenager raised a wary brow. "Don't shrink me, Mom. That's what you pay Dr. Bradford for."

I narrowed my gaze. "Well, do you? Do you want

a relationship with your father? And keep in mind, he's the only father you have." I wasn't above deploying mommy-guilt. "Your dad changed your diapers, coached your baseball and basketball teams. He attended every sporting event you ever played in high school. And he loves you," I said with as much gentleness as I could manage. "Now tell me, do you want a relationship with your father? Yes or no?"

"Sure," he said more than a little grudgingly. "But not with Coach."

"I'm not trying to make you have a relationship with Adam, but he and your father are a package right now." The words, even from my own lips, were a punch in the gut. Evan was a package with someone else now, and like Michael, I had to find a way to come to terms with it.

My teenaged son grunted. Unsympathetically, I clapped my hands to get his attention. "Get. Up."

"I hate you," he said through gritted teeth as he clambered from the bed.

I tried not to let the hurt show on my face. There were plenty of times I'd thought the same words to my mother when I was a teenager, but I never meant it, and I reminded myself as I let out a slow breath that Michael didn't mean it either. "You can hate me all you want, son, just as long as you mind me."

After dressing, and before he left the house, Michael gave me a rare hug and mumbled "love you" in my ear.

"I know," I said. "Love you more." And out the door he went. Once I was alone, my breath started coming faster, harder, and my pulse kicked up a notch—a feeling I knew all too well. This was the beginning of a panic attack. I tried to slow my exhales through pursed lips. *Blow out the candle*, I told myself, as I raced for the back door.

I quickly shoved it open and staggered into my floral paradise, aka my backyard garden. It was a brilliant mixture of colorful wildflowers and herbs. *Cleome and zinnias to attract butterflies and hummingbirds*, my mother had said when she'd help me plan the garden. There were yarrow plants for ladybugs. And fennel and dill, which are supposed to attract beneficial insects, but frankly, after all these years, I couldn't remember which bugs were good. I'd turned the fountain on in the spring, and the sound of trickling water started to soothe my anxiety.

I sat on a bench near a patch of garden phlox. The plants were all green now, but in July, delicate, pale-pink flowers would cluster in bunches. I put my elbows on my knees and lowered my head.

Linda stared at me with contempt. I flipped her off. She didn't react. Of course, she wouldn't. Linda was a stone garden gnome. I'd turned her around the night before, so she was staring at the dill and not at the bench. But—I was guessing—Michael had moved her to mess with me. The kid loved freaking me out. It was his new favorite game of let's see how many ways we can startle Mom.

Her beady eyes always creeped me out. More than once, I'd contemplated tossing her out, but she'd been a gift from my mother.

Every garden needs a gnome, she'd told me. *And this sweet girl will keep your garden lush.* Like a mini-Santa, the gnome had a snow-white beard. Mom had painted its hat and tunic pink.

"How do you know it's female?" I'd asked my mother.

"Oh." She'd given me a knowing look. "She's full of feminine energy." My mother had tapped her chest. "I can feel it in here."

I could've done without a gnome, but Mom loving the ugly statuette had softened my feelings toward the little creature.

"What now?" I asked Linda. "What do I do with my life now?"

I waited for a few seconds for a response I knew would never come. A rustle in the bushes drew my attention away from my stone nemesis. Two long ears twitched above a small rosemary bush, followed by the rest of the rabbit. It was much larger than an Eastern cottontail and smaller than a desert jackrabbit. I'd seen it several times since the beginning of spring, and I wondered what in my garden kept the little fella coming back.

I stood up and narrowed my gaze on my recurrent garden guest. "Hello, Bunny Foo-foo?"

The rabbit, reddish-brown in color, twitched its nose at me. The hair on my head and my arms raised as if the air had turned staticky around me. Only, there was hardly any breeze this morning. The rabbit scurried back behind some bushes, and by the time I walked over, I saw a burrowed-out spot under my privacy fence. The electric tingle I'd felt had disappeared with the small bushy-tailed beast.

I began to look up types of hares on my phone when it rang, saving me from going down that proverbial and literal rabbit hole. I smiled as the name of the caller flashed on my screen. It was my second to oldest sister, Marigold.

"Hey, sis," I answered. "What's up?"

"What are you doing tomorrow night?" she asked. No, how are you? No, sorry about your divorce. I loved that about my hippy-dippy sister. She knew how to avoid a sore subject.

I grinned. "I'm watching *Hospital Blues*. It's a new episode."

She sighed. "That's what DVRs are for. You can record it. Is there anything you can't get out of?"

I made a mental calculation of all the things I had to do this week, including anything involving work or Michael, and couldn't think of a darn thing. He was old enough now to drive himself to practices, and I'd finished editing "Don't Let Your Participle Dangle," a follow-up textbook to "Where Did I Misplace My Modifier?"

I used to be a professor of English out at Darling University, located just outside my hometown of Southill Village in the Ozark Mountains in Northern Arkansas near the Missouri border. I quit when Michael was born and had been working from home, living the glamorous life of a textbook editor ever since.

Unfortunately, I wouldn't have my next assignment until June tenth, so I didn't have a reason to say no to Marigold. "Is washing my hair a good excuse?"

Her tone was bright. "Not even in the slightest. Dress casual," she said. "I'll pick you up at four-thirty."

"So early? What are we doing?"

"There's an estate auction going on in New

Weston. We are going to bid on something eccentric and fun."

"We're going to do what?" I grabbed my coffee from the counter and sat down at my dining room table."

"Going to an estate auction. Ruth Boothwell died three months ago without any heirs, and her estate is auctioning off loads of fancy stuff."

"Fancy stuff, huh?" I asked skeptically. "Look, Mar. I don't have time to go to an estate auction."

"Come on, Iris. What else have you got planned?"

"Washing my hair. Shaving my legs. Waxing my mustache."

Marigold laughed. "It's about time. Self-care is the first step in reclaiming your life. But you can do that tonight. Besides, this is more than just a leisure trip. A colleague of mine, Professor Keir Quinn, has written a book and needs a good editor before he starts submitting it to publishers."

Marigold taught Women's Studies at Darling U. She, like me, had gone the academia route. This wasn't the first time she'd asked me if I would look at a "friend's" manuscript. The last one she'd asked me to look at had been a romantic thriller set in South Florida. I'd given it a hard pass.

"I don't know how many times I have to tell you that I don't do fiction, but...I don't do fiction."

Of course, I read fiction for pleasure, but I didn't want to have to ponder if a comma should exist in a sentence or if it was a choice the writer made to leave it out. Same with sentence fragments and other style issues that might or might not be on purpose. I liked the grammatical and mechanical clarity in which textbooks were written.

"I know you don't do fiction," Marigold shot back. "So, it's a good thing Keir's writing is of the non-fiction variety."

"Mills & Laden Academic Press sends me plenty of work to keep me busy."

She sucked her teeth, producing a sound of sheer annoyance. "I know you only get one book a month, and I also happen to know that you are amazingly fast at your job. Besides, you could use extra money right now, right? And this guy is willing to pay double your normal fees."

I sat down and closed my eyes as I prayed for patience, then asked, "Why would he do that?"

"Because Keir needs it done fast. You know how it is at universities. Publish or perish. Besides, it's an easy gig." My sister sounded exasperated with me. "You should take it."

"It's only easy if he's a half-decent writer."

"He is," Marigold assured me. "Look, come with me to the auction. Talk to the man. And if you decide to turn down the job, no harm, no foul."

The divorce, even with the sister-in-law lawyer discount, had been costly. I wondered if Rose had reached out to Marigold, and the two of them had cooked up this scheme to help me financially. I did need the money. And aside from that, even if I decided not to take the gig, going to an estate auction might be fun. The idea of getting out and doing something that wasn't work, kid, or husband —I shook my head at my mental slip—ex-husband —related stirred excitement in me.

"Fine," I finally said. "What time should I pick you up tomorrow?"

"I can drive," she protested.

"Barely," I told her. "Do you want me to go or not?"

I heard her harrumph. "I'll come over to your house at four, but you can drive," she said before I could protest. "The auction starts at five-thirty, but I want to get there early enough to check out the sale items."

"I'll be ready with bells on."

"Excellent," she said. "And Iris..."

"Yeah?"

"You know if you want to talk…about today or whatever, I'm here for you."

I nodded even though she couldn't see me. "I do know. Love you, sis."

"Love you back."

Read Earth Spells Are Easy today!
www.renee-george.com

PARANORMAL MYSTERIES & ROMANCES
BY RENEE GEORGE

Grimoires of a Middle-aged Witch
   https://www.renee-george.com/GMW
   Earth Spells Are Easy
   Spell On Fire
   When the Spells Blows
   Spell Over Troubled Water
   Ghost in the Spell

Nora Black Midlife Psychic Mysteries
   www.norablackmysteries.com
   Sense & Scent Ability (Book 1)
   For Whom the Smell Tolls (Book 2)
   War of the Noses (Book 3)
   Aroma With A View (Book 4)
   Spice and Prejudice (Book 4)

Peculiar Mysteries

www.peculiarmysteries.com
You've Got Tail (Book 1)
My Furry Valentine (Book 2)
Thank You For Not Shifting (Book 3)
My Hairy Halloween (Book 4)
In the Midnight Howl (Book 5)
My Peculiar Road Trip (Magic & Mayhem) (Book 6)
Furred Lines (Book7)
My Wolfy Wedding (Book 8)
Who Let The Wolves Out? (Book 9)
My Thanksgiving Faux Paw (Book 10)

Witchin' Impossible Cozy Mysteries

www.witchinimpossible.com
Witchin' Impossible (Book 1)
Rogue Coven (Book 2)
Familiar Protocol (Booke 3)
Mr & Mrs. Shift (Book 4)

Barkside of the Moon Mysteries

www.barksideofthemoonmysteries.com
Pit Perfect Murder (Book 1)
Murder & The Money Pit (Book 2)
The Pit List Murders (Book 3)
Pit & Miss Murder (Book 4)

The Prune Pit Murder (Book 5)
Two Pits and A Little Murder (Book 6)
Pits and Pieces of Murder (Book 7)

Madder Than Hell
www.madder-than-hell.com
Gone With The Minion (Book 1)
Devil On A Hot Tin Roof (Book 2)
A Street Car Named Demonic (Book 3)

Hex Drive
https://www.renee-george.com/hex-drive-series
Hex Me, Baby, One More Time (Book 1)
Oops, I Hexed It Again (Book 2)
I Want Your Hex (Book 3)
Hex Me With Your Best Shot (Book 4)

About the Author

I am a USA Today Bestselling author who writes paranormal mysteries and romances because I love all things whodunit, Otherworldly, and weird. Also, I wish my pittie, the adorable Kona Princess Warrior, and my beagle, Josie the Incontinent Princess, could talk. Or at least be more like Scooby-Doo and help me unmask villains at the haunted house up the street.

When I'm not writing about mystery-solving werecougars or the adventures of a hapless psychic living among shapeshifters, I am preyed upon by stray kittens who end up living in my house because I can't say no to those sweet, furry faces. (Someone stop telling them where I live!)

I live in Mid-Missouri with my family and I spend my non-writing time doing really cool stuff...like watching TV and cleaning up dog poop

Follow Renee!
Bookbub

Renee's Rebel Readers FB Group Newsletter

Made in United States
Troutdale, OR
02/29/2024

18072152R00125